The River's Price

The River's Price

Patren Blackmere

The River's Price

© 2025 Patren Blackmere

Published in Canada by Dream & Quill Publishing,

285 Geneva St. Fairview Mall Unit 1 Suite 1002

St. Catharines, Ontario, Canada L2N 2G1

www.DreamandQuill.com

Cover art by CANDesigner, 99designs.com

Paperback ISBN 978-1-0699730-0-9

eBook ISBN 978-1-0699730-1-6

Library and Archives Canada Cataloguing in Publication Data available upon request.

The River's Price is a work of fiction. Names, characters, places, and incidents are products of the author's imagination or are used fictitiously.

Dedications

To Amanda O. - for every page, every late night, and every reason to cross the finish line.

To Rose N. – who kept the fire burning when I couldn't see the light.

To Charlene O. – for all the visits that meant more than you knew.

And for the ones who still believe in real stories that light the path when needed most.

Table of Contents

Darkness is legion;

yet even legion cannot stand against the purity and will of light.

Carry it always; harmony is forged in shared strength and you are more important than you know.

Chapter One

All that lives was first imagined; and all imagined is Dream itself.

Mountains thrust themselves skyward, peaks briefly crowned in fire, only to subside as if exhaling into valleys before night could fall. Seas shouldered over the land and drew back again, leaving plains that cracked like old lacquer. Forests erupted in sudden green; their boughs hung with leaves that shimmered in brief glory, then fell to grey husk before a single fruit could sweeten. Even the heavens faltered: constellations spilled like forge-sparks across the vault, yet each star winked out as swiftly as it was kindled. What rose dissolved. What flowered withered. The world was flux without memory, a storm of becoming. Only the river endured.

Among those newborn wonders stood the Silver Forests, groves of pale-barked giants whose leaves were wrought like silver foil, thin and veined as if hammered by the hand of Dream. When the wind stirred, they struck against one another and rang like a thousand hidden bells. Sometimes a forest would stride a mile in a morning, roots lifting and setting like the feet of slow beasts; sometimes a grove would blur and thin until only the scent of frost and resin remained. They were beautiful, and they were faithless; they would not be told to stay.

Yet through that shifting country wound a river, clear as glass with a shimmer of blue, white-caps breaking at its bends. It is said the river was so pure that the first people beheld the stones at its bed glowing like lamps beneath glass. Along its banks the soil lay dark and heavy, close-pressed by grasses and moss. Where its waters ran swift, the earth was carved to sheer cliffs; where they slowed, they spread into pools that mirrored sky and forest alike.

From its surface rose veils of mist, drifting like pale spirits at the summons of its song. The river's voice was no single tone but a weaving of many, deep where currents pressed against stone, bright where ripples scattered sunlight, solemn where eddies circled in the shadows of overhanging boughs. At times its music seemed to gather into shapes half-seen, silhouettes of Dream itself leaning from the water to listen.

Upon its banks the first people awoke. They rose from mist and mud with wide, unknowing eyes. Their hands reached for earth and air as though to test the truth of themselves. When they stepped forward the ground heaved softly, and when they turned back, the path behind them had forgotten their feet. They learned by wandering, for there was no other school than hunger, cold, and wonder.

In those first days they followed shadows to find noon, only to learn that shadows changed their minds. They cupped water that slid away between remade banks. They chased deer that lost their antlers and became thickets; they reached for fruit that faded to ash before lips could close. They learned which grasses stroked the skin like silk and which cut like knives; which stones would sing when struck and which would crumble in the hand. They learned that the Silver Forests were fair but heedless, a branch might shelter them one hour and be gone the next. They learned to rest lightly, for the lands beyond the valley shifted like a restless dream, while the river country alone kept a steadier face.

Most stumbled blind through such treacheries. But Korain, lean and sharp-eyed, walked apart, his feet reading the soil as others read the sky. He could tell where grasses bent from the weight of deer, even when the animal had turned back into water, even when its hooves were swallowed by mud. "Look here," he told the younger ones, pointing to a print that deepened against the grain. "This ground lies, but not always well. If you listen, it will tell you where it stepped." They trusted him, for he alone seemed able to wring truth from land that shifted underfoot.

At the bends of the valley they raised cairns of flat stone, so that if the land around them changed, they might still know where to gather. When thunder spoke, they lifted their faces and learned the count between flash and drum. They learned to follow the river's shoulders, the little rises that promised safe footing, and to tread lightly where the earth turned black as ink.

At night, when the people gathered close, Seyra sat with strips of Silverwood bark in her lap. She split them deftly, twisting strands together, showing children how to cross and bind. "The land forgets," she murmured, "but knots remember." She wove three strands into one, crossing them twice before binding the end in a looped knot. She called it the Memory Knot, saying it held Dream and Flesh together. Soon others followed, tugging at one another's strands until the circle shone with knots and patterns, small anchors against the shifting world. The knot became their mark, a sign to outlast forgetting.

Through all of this one may wonder how the first people could have survived at all, but here lay the answer: Dream gave them fire. A strike of stone on stone cast a tiny star into tinder, and the breeze from the river's banks brought it to life. They stoked it with cautious pride, hands outstretched, faces gilded by its glow. Fire did not tire when the wind scolded it; it did not forget them at dawn. It warmed and warned, it cooked the flesh of creatures who lingered long enough to be caught, and it drove back the eyes that glimmered in the thickets.

Yet even in their awe they learned to fear it. A loosened spark could erase a morning's shelter; an ember fallen on a sleeping pelt could turn night to grief. More than once the wind carried flame into their drying grasses, and laughter at the hearth turned to screams. They learned to guard their kindling with stones, to scrape bare earth around their nests of light, to keep water close at hand. They fashioned bowls of wet clay to cradle embers from place to place, nursing each coal as a lifeline. They learned to speak softly to flame, as though to soothe a restless beast, for they had seen what ruin came when it wandered.

They learned to plait grasses into cords that held, for a time. To mark a meeting place by stacking stones, only to find the cairn sunk to pebbles by sunrise. They learned songs for rain that would not stay, and games for children whose laughter taught the fearful to smile. They mapped the country with their bodies: a scar to remember thorn, a callus to remember stone, a freckle to remember sun.

Among them was Selura, of average height and slight build, still young in her years and untested by hardship. She lingered by the riverbank where others did not, her wide gaze fixed on the current as though it carried a secret meant only for her. Her hair was dark brown, heavy and often stirred into loose strands by the river's breath, framing a face calm beyond her age. The ground seemed steadier beneath her feet, the chill of the shallows did not drive her back, and fruit that turned bitter for others stayed sweet upon her tongue. She moved with a quiet composure, her stillness uncommon among the restless.

Sometimes the river laughed; a quick, bright clatter over stones and the skin along her arms prickled as though called by name. Sometimes it lamented, deep and slow, and she felt her ribs stretch to hold a grief she could not place. At dawn it spoke like thin threads of glass; at dusk it draped like wool pulled long.

While Selura kept her vigil by the river, others turned inward to the fire. Not far from Selura was Iyren, older by a handful of years, a youth caught between boyhood and the shape of a man. Where she lingered at the river's edge, he lingered near the fire. It was he who crouched closest when Tharun showed them how to hold embers in clay, and from that night the flame never left his thoughts. His gaze followed the leaping embers as if they might reveal some hidden game. He was wiry and quick, eager to prove himself in tasks of strength, yet uncertain with words, his thoughts often tumbling faster than his tongue could shape them. The elders watched him with fond hope, for he carried promise, but already a shadow of restlessness stirred within him, not malice, only the ache of one who longed to be seen.

Veyra sat beside Iyren, silent more often than not, her black hair falling forward as she studied the embers. When others mocked his restless questions, she did not join them. Once she muttered, almost too low to hear, "The river shifts too often to be trusted. Better a fire in hand than a song in water." Iyren turned to her, eyes catching the flame, and gave a quick nod. It was the first pact of many, spoken not in vows but in shared silence.

And as the nights deepened, the people adorned their hair with braids by the firelight. Caregivers plaited strands for the young, friends for one another, even hunters for themselves, each twist a mark of kinship and hearth. Some knots spoke of lineage, others of bonds newly sworn. The braids shone bronze in the glow of flame, and by them the people knew who belonged, even when the land threatened to forget. Around the circle they laughed, teased, and sang, their hair a living record of fellowship.

Selura began to walk alone at grey-light, for in those hours the river's song seemed to change, shaping a tune she needed to hear again and again. Mist hung low in the boughs, and beneath the surface fish turned like thin blades, flashing and vanishing, as though they bore fragments of Dream in their scales. To others they were food; to her they seemed heralds, whispering of meanings she could not yet name.

She followed the riverbank where moss clung to stone and Silverwood roots dipped into the shallows. Sometimes she climbed the gnarled roots that leaned out over the water, crouching to listen as the river's voice rose differently from that height. The world shifted with her steps, yet the river kept its music, patient and unbroken. In that half-light her eyes seemed kin to the current itself: a dark grey band encircling irises pale as river-stone, within which flecks of silver, gold, fire, and rain glimmered faintly as though Dream had scattered its embers across her gaze.

The people watched Selura with a tenderness reserved for those who keep strange hours, though with it came unease. She was still a young woman, and the river's current was no gentle playmate. Now and then an elder would call her back from the shallows, fearing the pull of water or the bite of cold, yet she always returned when the dawn greyed again. They did not forbid her, some instinct held them back, but they spoke of her in lowered tones, half in wonder, half in worry, as though Dream itself had set her apart for a purpose none could name.

More than once, when children strayed too close to the current, it was Eshra's voice that pulled them back. Bent with years, her eyes clouded but sharp, she leaned on a staff of Silverwood and called, "Not so near, little ones. The river gives, but it does not love you." Most obeyed, but Selura lingered longer than the rest, and Eshra watched her with a mix of worry and reluctant wonder.

On a night of high wind and tattered moon, Selura lingered as she always did, her eyes set upon the river. Its song rose strange that evening, coiling around a single note that seemed to steady rather than wander. As she listened, it pressed upon her chest until her own throat stirred, as though a word, not yet born, waited there.

She bent low over the water, searching its ripples for meaning. Once, twice, she shaped the sound without letting it escape her lips, only a breath against her teeth. The syllable felt both hers and not hers, like something given and forbidden at once. In the hush that followed, she tried again, softer, and heard in it the faintest echo of the river's own cadence.

Others noticed. A young woman asked what she was murmuring. And Eshra, one of the eldest among them, turned sharply. Her hair was silvered as the forests, her shoulders stooped, her eyes clouded yet keen. She had lost two sons to the current and trusted it no more than a fire left alone. She spoke with a voice rough as bark: "Do not mock the river's tongue, young woman. What it sings, it sings for itself."

Selura flushed and fell silent, yet the word did not leave her. It clung, repeating in her ear as the water repeated against stone. She held it in secret, tasting it in her breath when no one watched, wondering if Dream had placed it within her.

So the first days unfolded; learning, losing, learning again. The people traced the newborn land with the soles of their feet, with the cups of their hands, with the heat of their gatherings. The river carried its patient music through all of it, blue-black and faithful where other things were not. Selura kept her vigil, still as a stone at the water's edge, listening until the listening itself became a kind of prayer. Somewhere beyond the bend, Dream waited with a word. And the world, unbound and unremembering, leaned a little nearer to hear it spoken.

Chapter Two

At first it was only a warmth behind the tongue, a coal cupped in the hollow of the mouth. Selura learned to carry it the way one carries water in two hands - carefully, without spilling. She did not let it fall into sound. At grey-light she stood where the bank made a clean lip over the river and shaped it without voice. When the sun and breeze found the Silver Forests and set their metal leaves to a faint chiming, she would turn away as though nothing had troubled her.

That first morning left her short of voice. By the third her steps felt heavier, it was as if the earth asked a small price each time she borrowed shape from its music. She hid these changes the way children hide bruises - without understanding what they mean, but knowing grown mouths will ask the wrong questions.

The people did not notice at once. There is always much to do when the world refuses to remember itself. Moss must be turned to bedding so it will forget the damp. Bark must be stripped in long clean ribbons for cord. Stones must be split to make a sharper truth from a dull one. Children must be kept from the clean drop into the river where the current darkens to a deeper blue. And fire must be kept - always fire must be kept.

When the day's tasks were done, Bren sat cross-legged by the hearth, his broad shoulders hunched as he threaded bone needles with thick fingers scarred by years of stone and antler. He grumbled to Mira, voice low and rough, "Selura grows thinner." Mira, older than most and listened to as an elder, did not look up from the tear she was mending. "She eats, but she still keeps fading," she murmured. "These days she feels more with the river than with us." Bren's mouth worked as though to answer, but he only bent lower over the needle, driving the thread through with more force than was needed. The fire popped between them, loud in the silence.

Eshra watched more closely. She alone seemed to see how Selura's voice shortened when the river's song ran strongest, how the girl pressed her tongue to the roof of her mouth as though holding a taste there. But Eshra had learned that warnings given too soon are taken for scolds. She said nothing the first day. Nor the second.

On the fourth morning, Selura turned from the bank, pale and unsteady. She pressed her tongue to the roof of her mouth as though holding back something that longed to rise. For the first time, she wondered if the word carried her as much as she carried it.

By afternoon the flush had returned to her cheeks, and she bent again to the day's tasks, laughing when a child's reed split wrong. For a little while she was only another pair of hands among them. When the others called her closer, she crossed to where Seyra sat splitting reeds for cordage, the elder's fingers moving with the ease of long habit. Selura lowered herself beside her, still shaken, and reached for the strands.

"The land forgets, but knots remember," Seyra said. "So do hands, if they are taught with patience. I know I say this often, but only because I want you to learn."

Selura smiled faintly. "I will be gentle with mine."

Seyra brushed a strand of hair from Selura's brow. "Gentle hands may be good for weaving, but the world will ask more of you, child. Sometimes you have to be strong, even when it hurts."

Near dusk, when the fire took hold and the Silver Forests began to glint like hammered sky, Eshra came to Selura and sat without calling for attention. They watched the river together until silence was no longer a thing to be kept but a thing already shared. "Would you tell me, what is it you do when everyone sleeps?" Eshra said at last.

Selura's shoulders made a small motion toward the water. "I listen to what the river tries to say. It calls to me, yet it is not clear.

"Your ears are not in your mouth," Eshra said gently. "I see you out there holding your jaw as if keeping a sound in."

Selura kept her gaze on the darkening blue. "There is a steady note in the river's song. It is steady when other parts wander. I feel, maybe, that if I can match that note, I could ask the world to hold a shape.

Eshra did not scoff. She had long practised tamping down her first answers, the ones that would turn truths to quarrels. "If a child found a way through the Silver Forests," she said, "whose way is it, the child's or the forest's?"

"Both," Selura said, and surprised herself by saying it. "If the forest did not stand, there would be no path. If the child did not walk, it would not be called a path at all."

Eshra's voice went out as if a tight binding had loosened. "You speak beyond your years, Selura. I will not try to stop you, but be careful. We do not know what the river might demand."

That night, a few paces from the circle of fire, Veyra and Iyren sat with a bowl of clay between them and a single coal voicing inside. Iyren's gaze wandered first to where Selura slept, her shape curled close to the embers, before he bent to the coal. "Do you think the river tells her things?" he asked. Veyra's hair fell forward as she studied the red. "The river talks to itself," she said. "If she hears it, she is in the right place." Iyren made a low sound in his throat. "I have sat by this fire until my eyes blur with smoke. It says nothing to me." Veyra glanced up. "It warms without words. Some gifts do not speak."

Iyren heard laughter rise from another hearth and looked away. He bent toward the coal, voice low. "It gives me nothing, no matter how long I watch." The ember flared once and settled, as if mocking him with its silence. He sat back with a grunt, and Veyra's eyes stayed on the fire though she said nothing more. Around them, the camp quieted into its last murmurs - children lulled by stories, elders weaving knots by firelight, the river still singing beyond the dark.

When dawn returned, the camp stirred with the small labors of survival: reeds split, bark stripped, stones carried to ring the fire. Selura's strength had returned enough to pull bark cleanly. She sat beside Seyra, who marked the rhythm of the work with an old tune - a song of Dream Lilies by the river, both fair and dangerous to seek.

"Down by the river the Dream Lilies grow,

silver on green where the swift waters flow.

Fair are their petals, twin-shaded with flame,

bright is their mirror that answers your name.

Step not too near though, the blossoms are sweet,

swift is the current that waits for your feet.

Those who would pluck them are taken away,

Dream keeps its flowers where strong waters play."

Children joined with their own fragments of the tune, circling dust with their toes. Selura found herself smiling at nothing - then at everything. The smile slipped when she reached to weave two strands and her fingers trembled where once they were sure. She set the cord aside and waited for her hands to steady.

Later, as reeds were gathered, Korain said, "The girl keeps to grey-light." He did not add which girl. None needed him to. Seyra's hands slowed on the strands she held. She looked toward the river, then back to her work. "She is careful," she said at last, softer than before. "That is more than most children. Sometimes the careful ones are the ones who walk the farthest."

"Careful is not the same as safe," Mira said, and pushed her mending needle through bark-cloth with a small click. "Her colour is thin."

"We know what you mean," Eshra said, and spared him the rest.

Eshra looked into the coals until the red deepened to a quiet heart. "I will speak with her," she said. "This calls for a gentle voice."

Selura tried again, half under her voice. The sound came rough, then rounded, as if the river itself had caught it and smoothed its edges before letting it fall back to her. The mist lifted in faint curls, and a hush seemed to lean close around her. She felt the word cling to her lips and linger in her chest, not heavy, but waiting - as though it asked to be spoken more fully.

That day the people noticed, for Selura stumbled where she had never stumbled before. Not all at once, but in twos and threes. A caregiver hissed a young child back from asking questions with a look. A boy named Daran, who admired Selura without hope, brought her water and placed it by her knee without speaking. Old Mira, who had never been cruel in her life and would not start now, offered a strip of dried meat and said, "Chew slowly," as if she were saying an ordinary mercy and not a benediction.

In the afternoon Eshra found Selura sitting with her back to a Silverwood trunk, eyes closed, hands open on her knees.

"You are counting your steps," Eshra said. It was not a question. Selura opened her eyes. "I am."

"Count smaller," Eshra said. "There are more of them than you think.

"If I count too small, I will never arrive," Selura answered, and both of them knew that was the truth and also the most dangerous lie.

That evening, when the circle drew tight and braids shone bronze in the light, a fuller talk rose. It did not begin with elders. It began with Bren the hunter, who could not help his plain mouth when worry sat heavy on it.

"If the river is doing this to the child," he said, "we should keep her from it. A week. A month. Whatever it takes. This is about her safety."

Selura heard him and kept her face toward the fire, because she had learned that faces betray more than words. Korain shifted where he sat. "And how would you do that?" he asked. "Will you post a watcher by her, or rope off the bank? Who will stop her when she decides to go?"

"Keep her from the river, then," Bren said, as if saying it could make it simple.

Seyra's voice came level and patient. "You cannot hold water with a rule," she said. "It will move anyway."

Mira looked at Selura and then at Eshra. "At least let us speak to her, not around her."

Eshra nodded and rose with the deliberate care of one who still wishes to be quick. She crossed to Selura and sat so close their shoulders shared heat. "Child," she said, no longer pretending the whole circle was not listening, "you are not alone at that bank."

"I never have been," Selura said, and lifted her chin toward the river. "It sings louder when I am tired. Or perhaps I hear it more when my strength is low."

"Does it ask anything of you?" Eshra's question was soft, the kind a caregiver would ask. Selura did not answer at once. At last she said, "Only that I be what I already am." She looked at her hands. "Which is strange, because that is the hardest thing I know."

A murmur of kindness moved through the circle then. Even Bren lowered his eyes. Mira reached across to touch Selura's arm. "Then stay close to Dream," she said. "If it sees you more fully than the rest, better to answer with courage than to hide in fear."

Veyra, who had said nothing, shifted the clay bowl closer to the centre and glowed the coal brighter for all of them. The ember flared, lighting the lines of Iyren's face.

He kept his gaze fixed on the spark. Around him, voices and hands turned toward Selura, and he felt the ground tilt as if she had taken the centre from them all. He told himself the coal was steadier than the river, that at least the flame stayed where it was set. Still, his jaw tightened. Why did Dream's song reach her and not him?

The next day did not pass as the others had. Selura rose with the rest, but she did not linger only to listen. She walked the bank with deliberate steps, testing her voice against the river's. First in whispers, then in firmer tones, she tried to give shape to the sound that pressed against her chest. Each attempt left her trembling, but she would not stop; the memory of the circle's kindness burned like a charge in her, and she felt she owed the word not only to herself but to them. Yet when the sun reached its height and fell again, the word had not answered her. She returned to the camp unsteady, her lips raw, the weight of silence heavier than before.

By dusk the sky lay torn with clouds across a half-moon, and the air had a sharpness that drove the people closer to their hearths. Iyren rose to gather fallen limbs, his stride quick as though the task were a race. Tharun met him halfway and steadied the bundle in his arms. "Not so tight," the elder said. "Wood needs air as much as we do." Iyren nodded, though he already knew it. He wanted more than to tend a fire; he wanted to master it, to prove his hands could command something that stayed when all else in the world shifted. He laid the wood as Tharun showed him, and when the flames caught, his mouth curved with pride - though he said nothing. Veyra, watching, dipped her thumb in water and smoothed the clay bowl's lip as if she could smooth Iyren's restlessness too.

The fire sank to embers, and the circle thinned until only voicing and the hiss of coals remained. Selura lay awake, the warmth fading at her back, the river's song pressing at her ears. Each time she closed her eyes she felt the word stir against her chest, as if waiting for her to unclasp it. Sleep never came.

When dawn unrolled its pale cloth across the river, she rose quietly and left the others in their mats. Mist still clung low, beading in her hair as she walked the familiar bend she had worn with her feet. She had meant only to listen again, to stand where the current held its many voices. But the river's hidden line no longer felt apart from her. It thrummed inside her ribs, a seam that demanded to be opened. She steadied her voice, her hands falling open at her sides. She knew the shape her mouth must make to draw it into the world. Knowing did not make the cost smaller.

She set her palms open at her sides and waited until her voice slowed. She thought of Eshra's counsel and counted small. She thought of Seyra's hands and the way knots held when crossing was true. She thought of Korain's way of reading ground and put her weight where the earth was thinking. She thought of Veyra's quiet, of Iyren's restless want for a language he could not hear, of Tharun's careful fire. Then she thought no more.

The first part of the word belonged to the front of the mouth. It was clean and exact. The second rolled deeper, a roundness set like a stone in the throat. The last was the hinge. She spoke it.

Sound went over water and into earth. It was not loud. But everything heard.

For a moment, the silver leaves ceased their chiming. The river's surface drew itself into a line, taut as a cord pulled straight. The bank did not crumble; it sank calm, as a sleeper shifting deeper into rest. From that stillness the earth parted, stone rising slow and deliberate. What had been mud shaped itself into arch and hollow, an opening that glowed cool air from within. Shadows pooled there, patient and unbroken, as though the land itself had opened an eye and chosen not to close it again.

Selura's strength spilled from her as if the word had been carrying her the way she had carried it. Blood warmed her upper lip and then fell in small red seeds upon the threshold. She swayed. Hands came - Eshra's first, then Seyra's, then Korain's and Mira's and even Bren's as if to make amends for the bluntness of his tongue.

"What is it?" a child whispered. "What do we call it?"

Eshra steadied Selura and did not take her eyes from the new darkness under the earth. "A place that stays," she said. "We will learn what to call it as we learn how to use it."

Korain stepped forward with the care of a man who has found a true edge. He put his palm to the threshold and then farther in where the air cooled. "It holds," he said. "It holds." He sounded relieved in a way that made the children listen and feel safer without knowing why.

Seyra ran her fingers along a ledge that grew from the wall, a stone shelf as if meant for keeping. "Here," she said softly. "Here we can set what must not be lost." She took a strip of Silverwood bark from her belt and, with Selura's shaky help, tied a Memory Knot that hung just within the doorway. "Bound," Seyra murmured, "so what passes has a place to land."

Tharun brought the clay bowl with a single coal and lifted it to send its patient light along the walls. Shadows rose and knelt, rose and knelt, as if learning a practice. "Not on the floor," Eshra said, and he nodded, holding the glow like a guest. Veyra stood beside him, her quiet steadying the ember more than any voice could.

At the mouth Korain placed three flat stones - one for each side, and one laid across them to teach eyes where the threshold began when fog or fear made minds wander. The children reached up to brush the stone above, then pulled their hands back as though it guarded the edge of a tale not yet told.

They did not bring flame inside that night. They learned the cave's voice first. The air moved neither quick nor slow; it kept its cool the way a promise keeps its time. Water beaded and remained beads. Moss that had crept there decided to be still. The river's song stood outside like a companion willing to wait at the door.

When they returned to the fire, the circle drew close without speaking of why. They shared fragments of memory and quiet concern, and Selura's name passed softly from mouth to mouth.

"What if there are more like it?" Bren ventured, almost gently.

"There will not be more yet," Eshra said. "We have only just learned the first step."

"What did it cost?" Mira asked, because someone had to say it. "And to whom?" She looked at Selura, her lips cracked and smeared with dried red, her tunic spotted where the blood had fallen. Her skin had gone the colour of ash, her eyes hollow and far-off, and still Mira did not look away.

Selura's chest still throbbed where the word had torn its way through. The strain was no longer sharp, but it lingered like a wound that would not close. Her hands trembled as she spoke. "It cost me," she said, her voice unsteady, "and not only me." She lifted her eyes to the circle, then to the river beyond. "It feels like I pulled a thread that runs through us all, and none of us can set it back again." No one told her she was wrong. No one told her she was right. They let the words lie the way one lets a net lie to see what will swim into it.

Iyren did not come to the doorway until the others had gone in and out again. He stood with the bowl lifted a little from his chest and looked at the mouth of stone the way a man looks at a mountain he has no idea how to climb. "She did that with a word," he said to no one and to Veyra. "I cannot even make a stick balance."

Veyra did not answer with comfort, which can make wounds angry. "You keep the ember," she said. "When the wind laughs, you keep it. When rain thinks she will win, you keep it. When your hands shake and the bowl feels heavy, you keep it." She touched the bowl with two fingers. "I keep it with you." Iyren's mouth made the beginning of a thanks and then shut. He did not want to give gratitude the shape of a small thing. He held the bowl more firmly instead.

By the third day, small offerings had gathered on the shelf: a shell with a hole through it, a shard of jet - a black stone that swallowed firelight instead of shining. The people left them in silence, glancing often toward Selura, who sat pale and watchful near the threshold. Her clothes still carried a scatter of dried red, she touched the marks as if to remind herself what had truly happened. At last, she spoke, her voice low and worn. "I do not know if there are others. If there are, they are not the same thread. I could not pull this one twice."

Eshra nodded. "One word is enough to teach the mouth that there are words." She leaned her staff against the threshold and looked outward. The Silver Forests flashed when a breeze found them and then grew still; the river slid past as if this had always been part of its plan. "We will be careful," she said, mostly to herself. "Careful is not the same as afraid."

Toward evening Korain taught a lesson no one asked for but everyone needed. He showed them how the ground nearest the cave had steadied, how the small slips that used to happen on the slope no longer happened. "Do not trust the ground," he said kindly. "Trust your feet. Learn where the ground is starting to hold." He tapped his heel twice and nodded, and half the children tapped their heels in agreement without knowing why their bodies were pleased.

When night came, the people braided one another's hair in the low light, the bronze of the plaits taking the fire and giving it back. They ate, and some sang, and a story about a fish that grew legs and then forgot how to swim made its slow circuit. No blessing was spoken over the cave. No law was made. And yet they behaved as if both had been given. Selura slept near the threshold again, this time with a rolled length of moss beneath her head and a pelt over her shoulders. When she turned in sleep, the strain in her chest moved like someone shifting to make room at a crowded table. It was not pain. It was not ease.

Iyren did not sleep quickly. He sat with Tharun after the last songs thinned and asked an honest question. "When you set wood and air together, do you ever hear a word?" Tharun thought for a time and then shook his head. "I hear work," he said. "Sometimes I hear thanks." Iyren rubbed his thumb along the stick he used to stir the coal. "I would like to hear thanks," he said, and felt foolish for having said it. "It is not foolish to want thanks," Tharun said, and then, to make the moment lighter, added, "If the fire ever thanks you, tell me first so I can run." Iyren laughed despite himself. Veyra, who had been listening without looking, let the corner of her mouth show she had heard.

Later, when his companions had ventured off to connect with Dream, Iyren sat alone by the ember's glow. The coals swelled and dimmed, then flared again, like a tide testing its reach. In the red, he thought he saw a narrowing and an opening that did not belong to the wood. He leaned closer, hunting a shape that might allow him to say: there, there is the line inside the fire. He did not find it. But he did not lose the wanting.

The Silver Forests stood pale, their bell-leaves hushed as though holding back speech. Between the trunks, shadows shifted, not deer, not wind, but Dream's strays that prowled when darkness deepened. Eyes glimmered and were gone. Once, a cry rose low across the river, long enough that every head lifted, though none could name the beast that made it. Their presence pressed close, but Iyren's thoughts clung to the ember before him.

At the threshold Iyren saw Selura lay still, her pale face turned toward the dark mouth she had opened. The people would remember her for this night, her name bound to river and stone, to a place that would not change. He had no such binding. He bent closer, willing the ember to answer, to grant him what the river had given her. But it only flickered, indifferent to his need. He saw again the blood at her lips, the ghost-pale of her skin, and knew the river had marked her with a price. Though the others honoured her for it, the weight of that cost shifted into his own chest. Why should Dream choose her pain to bind memory, and not his flame to hold it fast? The wanting stayed with him, sharp as the ember's glow, and colder still for the price he could not pay.

Chapter Three

The morning stood hushed over the Silver Forests. The leaves did not chime; even the river's song felt subdued, as though the weight of the first word pressed upon all things. Selura lay pale and enduring beneath a curtain of moss, tended by hands that brought her water and fruits. Their eyes turned toward her with reverence, unease, and gratitude: she, the doer of impossible things, had shaped a place that stayed. Yet the air itself seemed altered, thicker, as though watched by something unseen.

The stillness was not simple quiet, but like the land itself had craned to listen. The air seemed thicker, the ground steadier, as though both held some hidden watcher.

Already the world seemed to answer differently. The First People tended to offer sayings to each other before stepping out into the vast Silver Glade, "Walk with the light behind you," or "Keep your eyes on the path." Small words of courage, born of unease, none yet named aloud. As they returned they would whisper that the ground felt strange beneath their feet. They laughed uneasily, but kept their fires brighter at night.

The cave had grown into a world of its own. By day its mouth caught the light of the river, pale silver flowing over the stone, but within, the air was warm with fire and damp with moss. Beds had been laid thick across the floor, woven from reeds and river-grass, cushioned with the down of waterfowl. Children curled against them in small clusters, their limbs tangled as they drifted into sleep. Families marked their spaces with strings of shells and knots hung overhead, so that the faintest draft seemed to stir them like memory itself.

Near the fire, stones blackened smooth were set for cooking. The hunters laid out their catch, fish drawn from the river whose scales shimmered not in one hue but in shifting bands, silver, green, and violet, as though light swam beneath their skin. When split, their flesh glowed faintly in the firelight, a pale radiance that dimmed as it cooked. Fat sizzled on the stones and hissed into sparks, carrying a sharp, sweet scent unlike any flesh the people had known before.

Roots softened in the heat beside them, their skins cracking to reveal gold-threaded marrow. Hunters carved their kills with flint, telling stories of the chase, while laughter broke from the young who dared one another into boasts. Mira hushed the children when they drew too close, but her eyes carried a smile. Selura, pale but enduring, lay close to the fire, tended as though she were a flame that must not fail.

At night, shadows climbed the stone like living shapes. Some seemed beastlike, some winged, and the children whispered guesses as to which might linger when the fire died. Men and women sharpened flint, mended nets, or plaited reeds, the rhythm of their work steady as a chant. For the first time, talk of tomorrow wound through their gathering, fishing yet to be done, knots waiting to be tied, hopes of planting on riverbanks once the season turned. To the First People, such talk itself felt like a miracle.

Around the fire they began to speak not only of survival but of tomorrow. One voice suggested, "We could plant seeds by the river bend." Another laughed, "Maybe children born here will never know wandering." Laughter and hope mingled, fragile but real. Mira smiled as she listened, though her eyes betrayed the caution of one who remembered the wild's cruelty. In these moments, belonging felt possible, a dream made solid.

Hunters laid down haunch and pelt with ease, their shoulders lighter for knowing kin would be where they left them. Around the hearth, the people spoke not of moving at dawn but of weaving mats, storing meat, and teaching the youngest to plait cord for the growing circle of knots. For the first time, tomorrow had shape.

They were slow to trust it however, for none among them had lived in a world that stayed. Still, hope grew bold in their hands. Where once they woke expecting change with each dawn, now they laid moss with patience, believing it might greet them again tomorrow.

Still, the elders carried caution. When children pressed their cheeks to the stone and asked, "Will it walk away like the forests? Will it vanish when we close our eyes?" Mira placed a cup of water in Selura's hands and answered gently: "It is not like the forests. We called it, so it stays." Her words were steady, though her gaze lingered long upon the stone, as if waiting for it to crumble.

Beside her, Seyra tied a fresh knot to the threshold and said, "It will last if we care for it. If we remember it, it will stay." Her fingers moved deftly, nails darkened with resin from bark, but even she spoke with the careful tone of one who has seen too much vanish to give her whole faith to endurance. The children believed enough, racing through the cavern, delighting in its echo.

The people pressed close to Selura's resting place, yet their eyes wandered also to the cave that now sheltered them. She lay wrapped in moss-sheets, pale yet unbowed, her breath faint but steady. At her side, Mira kept watch, guiding children gently when they came forward with their newest knots. Selura's fingers, though weak, still curled around the threads they laid in her hands, and she managed the faintest smile as Mira helped her weave them into the greater line.

Around her, the cave had begun to change beneath their hands. Pebbles had been cleared from the floor, and along the walls rushes and fern softened the stone. Bren had climbed to the heights and broken a vent through the stone, so the smoke rose cleanly and the air lay clear. From that hour they named this flame the Homefire, their fire set within stone.

At the cave's centre, the Homefire, the small flame kept within the stone of their first home burned steady, its ring of river-rock chosen and set by many hands together. Hunters laid meat and river-fruit beside it with murmured thanks: "Your word held. We found our way back." Aravel bowed his head and said simply, "First home." The words passed from mouth to mouth like a blessing.

Knots dangled in bright rows, woven of bark, reed, and shell, catching the glow of the fire. Their colours shone against the stone, and in that shimmer the people felt their memories secured at last. For the first time, their laughter did not vanish into the wild but returned to them, soft and doubled, as though the walls themselves wished to keep their joy.

A small girl, bold with wonder, laid her palm against the threshold stone, cool beneath her hand, and whispered, "Will it stay for my children too?" Selura stirred faintly, lips moving but no sound escaping.

Mira smiled faintly, though her eyes flickered toward Selura. "I cannot promise forever," she said. "But it is here now, and it is strong."

For a moment the fire flared brighter, and the river's voice outside wove low and steady, as if keeping the same rhythm. For a time, the circle glowed with ease, voices mingling with firelight and the river's song. Hands touched stone, knots, and one another, as if to confirm the miracle was real. The first home held them, and in its keeping they dared to believe.

Iyren's place, however, was apart. He sat by the outer Hearthfire, feeding the coals with thin splinters, the smoke clinging to his cloak until he smelled more of ash than of man. His eyes burned from long nights staring into flame, yet no one turned to thank him for the watch he kept. Through the cave-mouth he heard rough verses rising, a song begun for Selura, halting but earnest, passed from voice to voice. Each refrain echoed back to him hollow, as though the stone itself refused to carry fire's name.

Shadows leapt across the inner walls, children laughing as they played among them, their faces bright in the glow of the fire. From where he sat, Iyren's own shadow stretched long and solitary across the threshold, swallowed by the dark.

The scent of roasting river-fruit drifted outward, sweet and cloying, reminding him of a feast where his place stood set apart, crouched by the fire rather than seated at the circle. Once, Mira's eyes caught his from within and she offered a faint smile, but he felt it land more as pity than regard. He turned quickly away, ashamed that he longed for more.

He told himself it mattered little. Flame was no less a gift, though the people treated it as a servant rather than a wonder. Still the thought clung like grit. The louder their voices swelled, in songs for Selura, in stories told by Aravel, the more he felt himself left in silence, shadowed by the girl whose whisper had shaped stone while his fire burned unseen.

By day, Iyren went into the Silver Forest with purpose, gathering wood that would take a spark, plucking river-sweet shoots, testing stones for their worth. Sun-thread filtered through the pale canopy and made the metal leaves look like coins shifting in a high breeze.

The paths were never the same twice. Dream's flux laid mirage upon mirage, and the ground seemed to lean away from his step. He marked his way with chips of bark and broken reed, yet the markers turned coy in the underbrush, drifting where they had not been. A child's rhyme flickered on his tongue, little words the people had begun to trade at the threshold for courage: "Keep to the bright, keep to the near; where mist grows thick, turn back from here."

He pressed farther than he meant to. The light thinned to lambent silver, and hush gathered under the trees as if a great shape held its breath. The air turned sour, rot braided with the tang of metal, and a wet, choking gurgle rose somewhere ahead, the sound of something drowning on dry ground.

Grass at his feet withered as if from a sudden frost. The silver leaves above him quivered to a high, metallic keen that set his teeth on edge. Mist pulled itself close, dense as wool. He turned to the clearer way, and the clearer way had slipped aside.

Something brushed his shoulder. Cold. Damp. As if a sodden hand had dragged across his skin. Iyren spun. Only mist. Only trunks lifting pale as bone. He called out once, a raw whisper, and the gurgling answered nearer, then no nearer at all, as if the forest itself moved the sound.

The forest bent around him in ways he could not follow. One moment the trunks stood straight, tall and silver-pale; the next they leaned as if listening, their bell-leaves humming at a pitch that scraped his teeth. The path seemed to shift beneath his step, roots snaking forward, reeds sprouting where bare earth had been. He blinked and thought he saw faces in the bark, hollow-eyed, half-formed, watching and gone.

Mist pooled low, and in it shadows slid like fish beneath a river's skin. His heart hammered; the air itself felt thick, as though the world were choking on its own breath. Then came the sound, a wet, guttural choke, too close, too human. A stench of rot pressed against him, and something damp brushed his shoulder. He spun, but the path was gone, the trees crowding close as if they had always been there.

The Silver Forest closed about him, vast and heavy. Grey trunks rose like pillars, broad and immense, swallowing what little light bled through the canopy. At times a pale gleam slid down their sides like a knife of light, then was gone. Above, the leaves shone like hammered silver, each veined with red and purple that pulsed faintly, as though blood threaded through foil.

Iyren pressed on, though the path bent under his steps. Roots thrust upward where none had been, tangling his ankles, while reeds sprang in sudden thickets that hemmed him in. Mist thickened low across the ground, acrid on the tongue, carrying a sour tang of mould. Every turn drew him deeper, the way behind vanishing as trunks closed and shadows thickened.

The air grew taut with sound. The silver leaves trembled until they gave a high, metallic whine that scraped the inside of his skull. Beneath it came another noise, wet, guttural, as though the forest itself choked on its own abundance. The mist stirred with it, curling into half-shapes with bleak faces that blinked out when he tried to look.

Then it came closer. A bubbling gargle, thick and wet, broke against his ear. His chest locked. The stench rolled over him, rank and putrid, sharp enough to sting his eyes. He reeled, dragging his cloak tight, but the rot clung, seeping into him.

Then it touched him. A brush across the back of his neck, damp, clammy, wet, like the skin of a rotting fruit that sweated its own foulness. Acrid reek rose sharp in his nose, burning his throat. The contact lingered, sinking cold into his flesh, as though consequence itself had laid its mark upon him. His cloak hung heavy with it, mildewed and damp, and his skin remembered even as the air cleared.

Through the fog two red embers burned low, steady, unblinking. They fixed upon him with hunger, not for meat alone but for the flux itself, as though the world's abundance was being swallowed, choked, undone before his eyes.

Iyren staggered back, then broke forward in panic. He tore through reeds that had not been there an instant before, clawed past branches that reached without wind. The ground sucked at his feet, pulling as if it would drag him down into rot. At last he burst from the trees, stumbling into the meadow. Clean air struck his chest, but his cloak still stank of decay, and though the forest lay behind him, unease clung to his bones as if hunger itself had followed him out.

The stench rode with him across the meadow, sour and clinging, as if the forest had laid a hand on him and would not let go. At the cave mouth children chased their shadows; within, voices gathered for Selura, the tune rough and warm, and nothing like the night he had crossed.

Mira stood by the water skins and raised a hand to stop him as the smell reached her. "Are you hurt?"

He steadied his voice and shook his head. "No, I am not hurt."

Her gaze travelled over the ash on his cloak and the tremor in his hands, and her tone stayed even. "Wash at the shallows. Then take the outer fire. Do not bring that inside."

He kept his eyes on the stones so his mouth would not betray him. "I will keep the watch. It will pass," he said, and heard the edge in his own words.

He worked the cloak in the shallows until his hands numbed. The rot thinned but did not leave; it lived in the cloth and on his skin. He set the cloak to drip over a low branch and settled by the outer hearth, where the coals held a steady glow.

After a while Iyren leaned toward the fire, seeking steadiness. He crouched low, whispering into its crackle as if it alone might understand. "I cannot tell them. There is no word for it. No name. Only the wet, the rot, the sound that does not belong." His voice shook; the flame only spat cinders, sending them upward like brittle stars. "They see you only as warmth, as servant," he went on, eyes fixed on the glow. "But I know you are more. I have kept you through storm and hunger. I have watched you dance when all else faltered."

He leaned closer, too close, drawn as if the blaze itself beckoned him inward. Heat flushed across his skin, but he did not pull away. Inch by inch he lowered his arm, yielding more than slipping, until the fire seized him. Flame licked up his flesh, blistering deep, the hiss sharp as sap in a green log. Smoke curled thick in the night air.

For a heartbeat his body convulsed with agony. Then something broke open in him. Laughter spilled from his throat, first raw, then ragged, then wild enough to shake him to his knees. He clutched his charred arm, trembling, but his eyes shone fever-bright. "Yes," he gasped between bursts of laughter, "yes, mark me. Make me yours." He rubbed at the wound as if to prove it real; when pain flared he laughed louder, a keening note no meadow had ever known.

The fire roared back at him, colours bending strange, violet and blue writhing among the red and orange, its sparks rising like script too swift to read. Iyren swayed with its rhythm, tears carving streaks through ash on his cheeks, his ruined flesh trembling above the glow. His voice unraveled into fevered murmur, half-sense and half delirium, as though he were both speaker and vessel.

"I will not fail you," he whispered, laughing still. "I will not be a shadow. I will make you greater than stone, greater than any word."

"Splinters," he muttered, "they do not last." Another crack. "Yes... too thin, too weak to stay. They vanish before anyone can see them." His hand clenched until the nailbeds whitened. He shot a glance toward the cave mouth as if fearful the others might hear him, then muttered again, "They are blind. All blind. Only I see what you are."

Smoke writhed above the stones, curling into knots too tangled to be chance. The patterns bent and folded, and in their twists he imagined meaning, a voice hidden in haze. He rose and paced in circles, his feet leaving black prints in the ash. He bent low again, his face so close to the flame that his lashes curled and singed.

"A coal dies too soon. Ash scatters, unseen. But permanence... permanence must burn with something heavy enough to stay. Something the world cannot ignore when it burns." His voice cracked. He whispered it once, then again louder, as though insisting upon a truth no one else would claim.

His gaze turned to the dangling knots within the cave. Their cords were bark and reed, feathers and shells, all woven with the care of the First People. The handiwork of children's fingers, the pride of elders who tied their years into cord. Iyren's mouth twisted with awe and envy alike. The fire snapped high, sparks clawing upward, and he laughed, high, breathless, fevered. "The knots. They hold us. They carry memory. They are what stays."

The blaze spat again, like laughter through smoke. Iyren fell to his knees, pressing his burned arm into the ash until black dust smeared his skin. He rocked forward and back like a man overcome. "Yes... yes. Burn them. Burn what stays. The fire will speak."

The fire answered with a sudden flare, sparks leaping sharp into the dark. Iyren's eyes widened. He laughed low, nodding as though he had heard.

That night, as the people slept, Iyren crept into the cavern's living quarters. His burned arm throbbed with each heartbeat, as if the fire's will beat within him. The knots hung heavy in the glow, swaying faintly as though alive. Their cords gleamed faintly, reed, bark, dyed thread, shells polished in the river's current.

He reached, and the sting of his burn flared again, sharp as rebuke, but his hunger drowned the pain. He whispered with each touch, "This one for flame. This one for permanence. This one for me." His words shook, but his grasp did not falter.

The memory-knots lay beside the fire, woven reeds and sinew braided as the people had done since the first days, darkened with dyes of berry and root. Threaded among the cords were slivers and beads of river-shell, cool to the touch, their pale faces notched and stained; here and there a feather or a shred of bark had been tied for luck. Each twist felt like a name made tangible, each crossing a day held fast, the whole a small weight of belonging.

Iyren's gaze fixed upon them and would not turn aside. He told himself he would only feel their weight, only learn what it meant to hold what stays, but the fire behind him snapped and flung a hot scatter of sparks as though it urged him on.

When his fingers closed, the knots resisted. The plaited fibres rasped his skin, and the edges of shell bit deep into his burned palm. Pain flashed and steadied there, not a warning but a brand, and he did not recoil. Breath ragged, he whispered that fire knew him, marked him, demanded more than scraps and splinters.

He drew the knots to his chest. They smelled of smoke and damp earth and the labour of many hands. Within them he felt the press of children's laughter, the patience of elders, the quiet pride of hunters returned. To take them was to wound the whole of his people, yet his ears heard only the rush and crack of the flames, as if the blaze spoke without words and all its speech was hunger: Give. Burn. Become.

Clutching the cords tight, Iyren turned from the fire with eyes fever-bright. The meadow seemed to tilt for his step. He no longer felt a youth in longing but a vessel borne forward, bent upon crowning flame as Selura had crowned stone. Whatever the cost, he told himself, he would not remain a shadow.

He cast the knots into the waiting blaze he had raised. For a heartbeat nothing stirred. Then, suddenly, the fire reared up as though gripped by a will not its own.

Flame twisted into colours no mortal blaze had ever borne: blue at the heart, violet tongues writhing above coils of red and orange. The air buckled with heat. A roar rose that was not mere sound but the rushing of power through the night.

The blaze writhed as though intent had seized it. Sparks scattered, and where they struck, grass shriveled black. Reed shelters caught as if they had long awaited fire's touch. The air warped, sight bent, sound trembled until everything seemed to tilt.

Then came a sound that froze every voice. The Dream Lilies at the meadow's edge blackened, their petals withering to ash. As they burned, they screamed, thin, keening wails not of beast nor man but of Dream itself in agony. The sound pierced bone, echoed through the river's song, and carried far into the forest.

Woken from slumber the people fell to their knees. Children covered their ears, but the cry burrowed deeper, inside the skull, inside the heart. Caregivers wept aloud, hunters shouted in despair. It seemed the land itself wept with the Lilies as they died.

The meadow's destruction spread. Insects dropped from the air, their wings scorched mid-flight. Small beasts darted from their burrows only to collapse, their fur alight. The reeds along the water burst like drums, exploding into fragments. The timber of the old shelters cracked and fell in pillars of purple-orange flame.

The fire moved with will, arcing toward the dwellings left behind, leaping as though guided. Sparks fell in deliberate arcs, finding new fuel. It did not spread like wild flame but chose, striking where it could wound most deeply.

Selura, still weak from her word, stirred at the cries. Her limbs trembled as she rose, Mira's hand bracing her elbow. Each step was a burden, yet she pressed forward, driven by the sound outside. Her hair clung damp to her face, her eyes wide with dread.

They emerged into the night. The meadow roared with fire. Colours clashed, violet tongues writhing with crimson, blue cores blazing sharp as ice. Selura gasped, the sound harsh and ragged, and pressed her hands to her ears, but still the scream of the Lilies entered her. It was not sound alone but anguish woven into the marrow of the world.

Daran, broad-shouldered, eager, his eyes always quick to the smallest cry, rushed forward through the chaos. A child stumbled near the burning shelter, her small hands flailing in the heat. Without thought, he darted to her, scooping her into his arms. Relief flickered across his face, then the shelter groaned.

A beam split and fell, glowing with violet flame. It struck across his shoulder, and fire leapt as if it had been waiting for him. For an instant his whole frame was rimmed in unnatural light, violet tongues coiling with red, and the air filled with the sharp hiss of flesh searing.

His cry rang out, sharp and terrible, joined by the girl's scream as she clung to him. He staggered, refusing to loosen his hold, even as the flame crawled down his arm. Bren charged through the smoke, wrenching the beam aside and beating at the fire with his cloak until it hissed and guttered. Together they pulled Daran free, the child slipping from his arms into waiting hands.

When the smoke cleared, Daran lay gasping, his jaw clenched tight against the pain. The skin of his shoulder was blackened and split, the smell of charred flesh heavy in the air. Mira dropped to her knees beside him, pressing moss against the wound with trembling hands. "Hold still," she begged, though tears streaked her soot-stained cheeks.

Children wept openly, and even the hunters stood stricken, their spears lowered. To see Daran, always the first to help, laid low by fire shook them as deeply as the lilies' scream. It was not only meadow and memory that Iyren's madness had marred, but the body of their kin.

The blaze consumed until it could burn no more, the meadow blackened and hollowed, then fell at last into its own ash. The people stood wordless, their world scarred before their eyes.

When the embers dimmed, the people gathered. Their eyes were red; their bodies streaked with soot. Seyra, bent with years, her hair silver-threaded, spoke first. Her voice shook with grief yet cut sharp as flint: "He betrayed us." Her hands trembled as she pointed at Iyren. Her whole frame seemed smaller beneath the weight of sorrow.

Aravel, tall and stern, his shoulders square as a wall, raised his voice. "Exile is not enough. He has burned our memory, and memory is who we are." His face glistened with sweat, his jaw clenched. "He has no place here."

Others joined him. A woman tore knots from her own wrist and cast them into the ash as though to mirror the ruin. Children clung to their caregivers, sobbing. Mira's voice broke as she wept softly, her hands blackened by soot, her eyes hollow with grief. "He burned our memory," she said. "What will hold us now?"

Selura stood pale among them. Her body trembled, yet her voice, faint, yet clear, silenced all. "We cannot sing it back," she said, eyes on the blackened stems. "I feel it with you. Hold to one another, see to the wounded, keep what remains. Let the night be for keeping and for quiet. In the morning we will face what this has made of us."

Aravel's face was carved hard as stone. "This was no accident. He took what was ours, what was meant to hold us, and fed it to ruin."

Seyra shook her head, her hands trembling though her voice was firm. "I do not understand, he was not always like this; I have seen him watch the flame with care. Something has changed, a sickness of the mind maybe, or a shadow in the world; I cannot say."

Mira, standing near Selura, said nothing at first. When she spoke, it was low, bitter. "We were warned. Nothing is given without cost. The stone we were given, the home we found, all demanded an answer. We thought the river's gift would suffice, but now fire has claimed its price."

Iyren stood apart. His eyes glowed fever-bright, his burned arm smeared with ash. Some surged forward, fists raised. But Bren, broad as two men, his beard coarse, his voice usually mistaken for wrath, barred the way. He lifted a hand like a shield. "No," he said, low but carrying. "If we cast him out, the wild will finish what the fire began. Better he stays where we can watch him."

He turned his gaze upon Iyren, eyes dark with sorrow, his presence commanding. "What set you to do this, boy? You are not the Iyren I know."

Iyren did not lower his eyes. He looked through Bren to the embers, as if the glow were a face only he could read. "It called," he said, fever-sure. "Knots held us to yesterday; I gave the fire what stays so it would keep us. The stone holds quiet. Fire holds our vow." He raised his burned arm and did not flinch. The circle tightened; two hunters came to either side but did not touch him, and he stood under every gaze. For a time no one answered, and then the camp turned to keeping. Water passed hand to hand, ash gathered, Daran carried in, while Iyren remained fixed to the ember light like a nail set in iron.

Thus, the first home endured, though scarred. Selura's word had bound stone to stillness; Iyren's fire had unbound memory to ash. The meadow lay blackened, the first dwellings gone, and a wound smouldered where laughter had once risen. Yet the cave stood, and the river sang on, carrying both hope and grief.

Elders sat in stillness; their eyes fixed on the ground as though seeking meaning in the dust. The river, though it still sang, carried a lower note, subdued beneath the weight of what had been lost.

In that night the First People learned a harsher truth: what is shaped will be marred, what is given will be answered. They did not name the shadow then, but they felt it near, heavy as breath against their skin, waiting. And from that hour it was said; nothing without cost.

Chapter Four

Rain came before morning. It fell soft at first, hissing where it met the embers, then steadier, drawn from a sky the colour of old iron. The meadow breathed smoke through its wounds, thin threads rising and twisting before the rain claimed them. Heat still lived in the ground, steaming where drops struck, the scent of copper and burnt lilies thick in the air.

Dawn edged over the valley without colour. Water pooled in the furrows of ash, turning the black soil to mirror. The reeds where lilies once grew bowed under the weight of it, their stalks glistening like wire. The world lay raw and glistening, a wound that had not yet decided whether to heal.

The river fights itself. Currents reverse and collide; waves slap the banks in weary rhythm. Its voice, once the song that lulled the valley, is now a broken hum too deep for comfort. Selura feels it before she hears it: a tremor through the soles of her feet and up her spine until her teeth ache. She steadies herself on a charred trunk. The water carries Dream's will, uneven, pulled thin.

Mist rises where heat meets falling water, silvering the scarred meadow. What was green now gleams slick grey, a skin over bone. A child's toy, half a reed flute, lies melted into the mud. The world that had sung is silent save for the rain's slow whisper and the murmur of cooling earth.

Selura moves through the ruin as if through fever. Each step sinks, the ground hot enough to smoke against the rain. She thinks she can still hear the lilies screaming under the soil. Around her the First People gather in twos and threes, stunned, raw-eyed. No one dares to call this morning. They only wait for the world to tell them it is finished.

It is Bren who first dares the heart of the burn. The giant's shoulders glisten with sweat and rain. He uses a branch as a staff, prodding at glowing patches until the hissing fades. Steam curls around him, hiding his face. "It is dying," he says at last, voice flat with disbelief.

Selura closes her eyes and listens beyond his words. The river's tone shifts again, less rage, more pain. Its pull tugs at the ash as though trying to draw it all back into itself. She whispers, "Dream, let go," and the water shudders in answer, sending a fine spray into the air that beads on her lashes.

By midmorning the last tongues of fire sputter out. Rain settles into steady rhythm, heavy enough to soak through soot to soil. The meadow exhales a sour heat, and steam covers the bodies of burned trees like frost's memory on glass. The blaze that had devoured their world dies without witness but the weary. The silence that follows is not peace; it is disbelief made visible.

Selura kneels, pressing a palm to the blackened earth. The texture is wrong, soft where it should be firm, the hum of Dream faint beneath. When she pulls her hand away, soot stains her skin like ink. She looks toward the river. The current slows, as if exhausted by its own grief. For a moment, its voice steadies into something almost kind, and she understands it has spared them, barely.

Behind her, Mira coughs the smoke from her lungs and begins to call names. Daran answers hoarsely, alive but trembling. Others answer one by one until the roll call becomes a prayer. Iyren's name no one calls. He stands apart, his shadow long against the cooling ground, watching the smoke drift east.

The rain thickens again. Selura lifts her head, tasting it, and feels the ache of the world settle on her tongue. Around her, the people sink to their knees, not in worship but in sheer weariness. The meadow hisses once more, then falls still. Only the river keeps speaking, low and wounded, carrying the first ashes of the First Fire toward the sea.

When the sound fades, she realises the world is breathing differently. The air smells new, as if the rain itself were testing what it means to exist. Selura draws the smoke-sour air in shallow sips. She is not the elder they look to, not yet; she is a girl with ash under her nails and river-water cold in her sleeves. The world around them still feels half-dreamed, unfinished, each breath a reminder that creation has not settled. If she speaks wrong, the silence will devour them; if she speaks not at all, it will do the same. She rubs her thumb along a splinter in her palm until a bead of blood forms, proof that she is real in a world that still questions its own substance. Veyra stands nearby, watching the horizon as though she might catch the world changing again. Selura straightens anyway. There is no one else to lift them to standing.

Rain holds through the afternoon, thin and cold, washing the last smoke from the air. When the survivors move again, it is not from courage but from habit, the body remembering what to do when the heart cannot. Bren leads them across the wrecked meadow, boots sinking deep into soot and mud. Behind him, the others follow in a ragged line, faces grey with ash.

Cold creeps into the places the fire missed. Hands tremble when they lift what little remains. The water Bren passes tastes of stone and ash, yet they drink, letting it scald their throats with cold. A child's teeth chatter. Mira wraps her scarf around the small jaw, her fingers shaking. Every sound feels too loud: reeds snapping, cloth tearing, the wet click of burned bark underfoot. They move anyway, because stopping would give fright a voice.

Veyra walks a half-pace behind, her eyes working where words cannot. She counts without counting: who limps, who hides a wince, who stares too long at the ruin of the knot walls. When a cord-end half-buried in soot catches the light, she nudges it toward Seyra's basket, no claim, no call of discovery, only the quiet habit of gathering what might still matter. She watches Iyren the same way she watches the treeline: not to judge, not to forgive, but to learn what danger looks like when it wears a human face. If anyone asks later what happened here, she will be able to say it true. That is her only oath.

The meadow is unrecognisable. Where reed huts and woven walls once stood are mounds of cinder and puddles that mirror nothing. The air hangs thick with the metallic tang of spent fire. Each step stirs the smell anew. Mira ties a strip of cloth across Daran's mouth and shoulders his weight when his burned arm fails. His eyes are wide and unfocused, the look of someone who has seen too much light.

Selura keeps pace beside Bren, naming the missing as if calling them might weave the world back together. Each name answered brings a breath; each silence cuts another piece away. When she reaches the end, nine names have no reply. The number hangs between them like smoke that will not rise.

"Careful here," Bren calls. The ground near the river's bend has caved where the fire burned the roots beneath. He hauls aside a half-collapsed frame, revealing what was once a knot wall. The braids are gone, only blackened fibres clinging to stone, the pattern burned out of memory itself.

Seyra falls to her knees and lifts a handful of ash, the record of their lives. It drifts apart between her fingers, grey dust running down her wrists. "It is all gone," she whispers. "All of them."

The others gather close. Some kneel, some simply stare. Even Bren is silent. Selura presses her fingertips into the ash as if testing for a pulse. The ground is cold beneath. Dream's hum, once constant, feels distant now, as though it too has forgotten their language.

Mira looks skyward. "The river still runs," she says, voice trembling. "We can follow it."

"Follow it where?" someone asks, but no one answers.

The sound of the river fills the space that follows. Its tone is quieter now, not rage but grief. Selura listens to the broken rhythm. "I think Dream mourns with us," she says softly, though she does not sound certain.

Bren straightens, rain sliding down his face. "We move what we can to the cave," he says. "If it still stands." His voice leaves no room for argument. The people rise and gather what remains: bundles of reeds, shattered tools, anything that still holds shape. The meadow groans under their steps, as if the earth itself protests being touched again.

Iyren lingers at the edge of the group, staring where the knot walls stood. Veyra glances back once before following the others. When she is gone, he stoops and presses a handful of ash into his palm. It stains him instantly, impossible to wash away in the rain. He closes his fist around it until his nails cut skin, then lets it fall. The river wind takes the dust and scatters it east.

The rain eases by the time they reach what was once the Hearthfire. Smoke still curls in thin, colourless threads from cracks between the stones. The pit glows faintly in the dim light, not orange or red but blue-white, as if the rock itself remembers burning. The air here is strange, cold and heavy, humming like a distant drum. It smells not of wood or soot but of metal and salt.

Bren halts at the edge. "No one cross the ring," he warns. His tone carries weight enough that even the children freeze.

Selura steps closer despite him. The fused stone pulses in rhythm with her own heartbeat, each flash of pale light followed by a whisper of heat that is not heat at all. It is a presence, wrong, familiar, yearning. The ground under her feet vibrates with Dream's dissonance. She steadies herself and peers into the pit. Beneath the glassy crust, shadows move like veins of smoke in water.

Iyren pushes forward. "It should have burned through," he says, voice cracking. "That was the point."

Bren's hand closes on his shoulder, dragging him back. "Enough."

But Iyren barely hears him. "It was speaking," he mutters. "It wanted out. I only opened the way."

Selura turns toward him, rain dripping from her hair. "And it devoured everything that listened."

The words land heavier than she intends. He flinches, looking down at the molten pit, and the reflection that stares back at him is wrong: eyes like coals, mouth a wound of light. He staggers back into Bren's grip.

Eshra arrives, leaning on her staff. She studies the warped stone, her expression unreadable. "This is not Dream's shape anymore," she says quietly. "Something else pushed through the flame."

The glow brightens, a single pulse that throws pale light across their faces. For an instant, every shadow moves in the wrong direction. Then the light fades again, leaving the circle darker than before.

Seyra touches the knot at her wrist and whispers, "It is cursed."

Veyra, still at the edge, shakes her head. "He did not understand what he was calling," she says at last. Her voice trembles, not with defence but with disbelief. "He thought it was only fire."

No one answers. The rain resumes, softer now, and steam rises from the pit in slow threads. The hum deepens, then dies, like a sigh beneath the earth.

Selura looks down once more. "We leave it," she says. "Dream will cool its own anger." She feels the river stir behind her, its song still muted but calmer, as if in agreement.

Bren nods. "No one touches this place again." He casts one last glance at Iyren, whose face is unreadable: grief, disbelief, guilt bound so tightly together they are the same thing.

They turn away one by one. Rain slides across the blackened glass, carrying ash into the river's mouth. The current swallows it without sound. When Selura looks back, the light within the pit has dimmed to a single glimmer, faint as a dying star.

By the time they reach the cave, the light is fading again. Damp clings to their hair and sleeves, streaked with soot. The path up from the river is slick and steep; twice Bren catches a child before they slide back into the water. The cave mouth glows faintly with the reflection of the Homefire, steady and untouched. Its survival feels like a miracle none of them are ready to trust.

They gather in the clearing before the entrance. The fire's glow flickers across wet faces, painting them gold and grey. Bren calls the roll, his voice echoing against stone until the shortened list falls silent. Only the drip of water through leaves answers.

Daran sits wrapped in Mira's cloak near the rock wall. His shoulder is bound tight with damp linen. Every few breaths he winces, muttering that he can still hear the lilies screaming beneath the ash. Mira hushes him, pressing a cup of river water to his lips. "You are safe now," she says. The words are gentle, meant to soothe more than to tell truth.

Selura moves through the group, checking wounds, pressing hands to brows, whispering small comforts too thin for the weight they carry. The people obey her touch, grateful for direction, for any sign that someone still hears Dream's will. She feels the faint warmth beneath their skin. Life remains, but it is fragile.

Iyren stands apart from them all, half in shadow. He has not spoken since the pit. Damp clings to his hair where soot once lay, streaks dark as scars. Bren watches him from the edge of his sight; his patience holds, but the muscle in his jaw tightens when Daran lifts his head.

"You did this," the boy says hoarsely. "Fire-thief."

The word cuts through the hush. For a heartbeat no one moves. Iyren does not answer. Bren's eyes find Daran's, hard, and warning. The boy's mouth closes, fear settling where anger had burned.

Selura steps between them. "Let it end here," she says, her voice low but certain.

The moment breaks. Daran trembles. Mira gathers him closer, murmuring to keep him still. Bren turns away first, his great shoulders slumping under the weight of command.

"We will bury the ashes before sunrise," Selura says. "What we lost deserves rest." Faces lift at her words. The promise of doing something, anything, steadies them.

Mira nods. "I will help." Others echo her softly. Even Seyra's hands stop shaking long enough to tie her hair back.

The Homefire glows steady, its warmth reaching the edge of the circle. Outside, the river hums a quieter note, the melody of something beginning to mend. Selura looks toward the dark line of trees. Somewhere beyond them lies the fused Hearth, the place where the fire burned too long, still glowing faintly beneath the mist, the wound of Dream cooling under the night.

Inside, the people move again, slow and dull-eyed, feeding the fire and one another. Iyren remains still, his gaze fixed on the ground. Veyra hovers near him, saying nothing. The unspoken truth hums between them: he is alive only because Bren wills it.

When Selura finally sinks beside the fire, exhaustion trembles through her arms. The light paints her hands the colour of new embers. "Tomorrow," she says, more to herself than anyone. "Tomorrow, we begin again."

The cave holds its warmth through the night, but sleep comes thin and broken. The survivors lie close to the Homefire, listening to its quiet pulse. Outside, the valley breathes in slow, uneven rhythms, the world cooling after its own fever. Selura dreams of rain turning to glass, of rivers folding back on themselves. Somewhere in that half-sleep, the wind shifts.

At the edge of hearing, something inhales. Not bird, not wind, a wet drawing in that stops the instant anyone stirs. The Silver Forest stands beyond the river with every bell-leaf stilled, as if listening back. Cold air slips from between the trunks and folds around the valley like water. The river lowers its hum by a note, warning itself, or them. Selura cannot name the shape of the unease, only feels her body turn away from it like iron from frost. Bren feels it too; even in sleep his shoulders tilt toward the cave mouth. The night watches, and the people do not see it.

Before dawn, the mist still lingers, thick in the hollows, thin where the wind has touched it. The air is heavy with the scent of wet ash and earth. When Selura steps outside the cave, the sky has begun to pale, neither night nor morning, only the colour of smoke remembered. The survivors follow in silence, their movements slow and deliberate, as though the weight of grief clings to their bones.

They follow the river's curve back to the meadow. The ground lies soft and dark beneath their steps, streaked with soot where the fire once ran. Mist clings low along the banks, the wind carrying an eerie whistle through the reeds. Each step feels like trespass, as if the land itself mourns what was lost. The fused Hearth waits for them, its last glow pulsing faint beneath a skin of cooling glass.

Seyra carries the baskets filled with the gathered ash of the knot walls. Her hands shake, but she holds them steady, knuckles white against the wicker. Aravel bears a spade carved from bone. Bren walks behind them, silent sentinel. No one speaks; only the river's rough murmur keeps them company.

At the centre of the ruined meadow, they stop. Aravel drives the spade into the softened ground. The earth opens easily, as if ready to receive what they offer. He digs until the pit reaches his knees, then steps aside for Selura. She lowers the first basket, ash spilling over her fingers. It drifts into the hole like fog, vanishing into the soil. One by one the others follow: children, elders, even Daran with his bandaged arm. The air fills with the soft hiss of ash meeting damp clay.

When the last basket is emptied, Selura kneels at the edge. She ties a single cord of grass and soot, thin, uneven, imperfect, and lays it atop the mound. "For memory," she whispers. Her voice is unsteady but holds. "For those Dream carried away, for the names we cannot find, and for the lines the fire unmade."

Mira lowers her head. "For Korain," she murmurs.

Bren's jaw tightens. "For Tharun."

The sound fades. Selura presses her palm to the cord. "They are not lost if we remember."

Aravel sets his broad hand over the knot, sealing it into the mud. "No speech by flame till sunrise," he says. The words come unbidden, heavy, and certain, as though the earth itself demanded them. The people bow their heads in agreement. Around them, the air folds in close, muting the world.

Iyren stands apart, just beyond the circle of mourners. His shoulders are hunched, his expression unreadable. Veyra's eyes find him, but he does not meet them. The distance between them feels wider than the river.

Bren turns slowly, scanning the group. No one moves. The moment holds, a stillness deep enough to hear the cave wind far behind them. Then the mist thickens again, gentle and cold, flattening the mound until it gleams dark as obsidian. The scent of wet earth rises, washing away the last tang of smoke.

Selura stays kneeling, watching rivulets form across the grave's surface. "Dream, carry them," she murmurs. Her words vanish into rainless air, but the river answers with a low sigh, steady and sorrowful. The sound carries through the valley like a lullaby for the lost.

When she finally stands, dawn has found them. A faint light spreads along the horizon, pale-gold on the river's skin. Bren touches her shoulder once, a gesture of respect, not comfort, and nods toward the path. "Come. The fire waits."

They leave the meadow behind, each step pulling their shadows longer across the wet ground. The new day rises grey and tired, but it rises all the same. Behind them, the mound of ash and memory steams in the early light, and for the first time since the fire, the wind smells faintly of rain instead of ruin.

Night does not end so much as it thins. The air at the cave mouth is cool and clean, carrying the faint scent of stone and soot. Inside, the Homefire burns low but steady, its light resting against the walls. The people lie scattered near it, too weary for speech, the promise of dawn a pale smudge beyond the vent above.

Selura cannot sleep. The image of the ash mound haunts the backs of her eyes, the grey soil, the knot sinking into mud, the sound of earth closing over memory. She rises quietly, drawing her cloak around her shoulders. Bren stirs but does not stop her; he knows the restlessness of grief.

Outside, the world holds still. Mist ghosts along the valley floor, thin as smoke. The meadow lies beneath it, silent and slick with dew. Selura can smell the fused Hearth from here, that faint metallic tang of stone cooled too quickly. Somewhere to the east, a branch snaps, a sound too sharp for the hush.

Iyren stands beside the fused pit. The glassy surface mirrors the dim sky, streaked with silver where condensation runs across it. He has not moved since the burial. Mud clings to his boots; ash stains his hands. When Selura approaches, he does not turn.

"I thought you had gone," she says.

He shakes his head. "Not yet. I needed to see it once more."

Selura looks down into the pit. The faint blue glow within has dimmed to almost nothing, but a whisper hums beneath the surface, the dying echo of fire that will not die clean. "Dream settles," she says. "It will find its balance again."

Iyren gives a small, broken laugh. "Maybe Dream will. I will not."

A voice drifts from the shadows near the trees. Veyra steps forward slowly, mist catching in her hair. "Then leave before what is left of you fades with it."

He glances at her, startled by the edge in her tone. "You think it matters?"

"It matters to me," she says. The words hang there, trembling. She does not reach for him, and he does not move closer.

The river's hum deepens, wary, as if Dream itself listens. Selura glances toward it. "You should not linger here."

Iyren nods. "I know." He looks at his hands, the thin black crescents beneath his nails. "There is nothing left for me here."

From the slope above, Bren's voice carries low and steady. "If you are going, go east. Follow the river until the ground turns red. Beyond that, no one will follow."

Iyren turns toward him, the fading firelight catching in his eyes. "Thank you," he says. The words sound foreign, like something borrowed.

Bren does not answer, only nods once and steps back into shadow.

Iyren bends to collect his small bundle, a knife, a flask of river water, a torn strip of cloth still marked with soot. He ties them together and slings the bundle over his shoulder. Veyra stands watching, arms wrapped around herself, lips pressed white. When he passes her, she speaks again, barely above a whisper. "Do not learn from darkness what fire already taught you."

He stops, half-turns as if to reply, then only nods. Moisture beads along his lashes, indistinguishable from the mist. He crosses the meadow toward the Silver Forest. Between the trunks, a pallid glow flickers, light without warmth, calling him onward. He hesitates once at the threshold, then steps into the trees and is gone.

Selura watches until the last trace of him vanishes. The forest seems to swallow its own sound after him. She stands a long time in the stillness before turning back toward the cave. The river hums low, and in its cadence she hears both mourning and relief. The balance has shifted, but not yet settled.

When she re-enters the cave, Bren has returned to his place beside the Homefire. The flame steadies as she passes. No one asks about Iyren. The people sleep on, their breathing shallow but unbroken. Selura kneels before the fire, holding her palms toward its warmth. The glow climbs her fingers, soft and gold. She closes her eyes and lets the sound of the river fill the silence, a single, endless current carrying through Dream's night.

For a moment, the valley holds still. The river skips a beat. Across the ash plain, light bends, like frost's memory on glass, and is gone. Selura lifts her head, certain she has heard a word too soft to live in air. The Homefire answers with a small, steadying rise, as if to say: not yet. Far to the east, a metal leaf chimes out of rhythm, a single clear note. Veyra notices and says nothing; she files the sound away with the rest. They step into dawn with their hands empty and their work heavy. Behind them the mist pulls itself flat, and the river's hum resumes as if nothing had paused at all.

Dawn comes pale and colourless, sliding across the valley like mist on glass. Mist clings to the meadow, silvering the black soil and the glistening stone. The world smells of steam and wet clay, a scent almost clean. Inside the cave still holding, the Homefire rests low and steady, its light painting amber halos on soot-dark walls.

The survivors wake slowly. No one speaks at first. Bodies stiff from cold, they pull themselves upright and gather nearer to the warmth. The glow touches their faces, revealing exhaustion cut with disbelief. They are alive, though none yet know what that means.

Selura remains seated before the flame. Her hands hover near the bowl's edge, feeling its quiet pulse. She can still hear the river outside; its rhythm softened to a lull. When she closes her eyes, she sees again the fused Hearth, the glass veins cooling, the shimmer of light slipping beneath the surface. The image fades, leaving only the warmth on her palms.

Mira stirs the embers with a stick, coaxing them higher. Sparks drift toward the vent above, lost to the early light. "It held through the storm," she says softly. "Dream still moves beneath it."

Bren nods but does not answer. His gaze lingers on the cave mouth, as if expecting Iyren's silhouette to appear against the grey. When none does, he turns back to the fire. "We keep it burning," he says. "For them. For us." The words carry the weight of stone laid into place.

Daran limps closer, his bandaged arm pressed to his chest. He kneels near the fire's edge, watching its reflection tremble in the water pooled at his feet. "It is quieter," he whispers. "The world."

Selura looks to him, then to the others gathered in the half-light. "The world remembers," she says. "That is why it hurts."

Veyra sits apart, back against the wall, eyes fixed on the flame. She has not spoken since Iyren left. When Selura meets her gaze, the younger woman looks away, drawing her knees to her chest. Selura says nothing more; some grief cannot be shared.

They eat what little remains of their stores: roots boiled in water, a handful of berries saved from before the fire. No one complains. The act of eating itself feels like defiance, a promise to the earth that they will endure. When the bowls are empty, Mira rinses them with water and sets them by the wall to dry.

Selura rises at last. She steps to the cave mouth and looks out over the valley. Vapour drifts in ribbons above the river. Where the Hearth once burned brightest, a faint green shimmer glows beneath the surface ash, new shoots already pushing through the ruin. She feels the ache of tears and lets them fall, quiet as dew through ash.

Behind her, Bren adds another branch to the Homefire. The flame accepts it with a low hum, its light reaching farther into the dark. The people draw nearer without speaking. Together they watch it hold steady, moving with it, finding rhythm again.

Outside, the river carries the ash of their past toward the sea. Inside, the Homefire endures. Dream's rhythm, once fractured, hums faint through the stone. The world has not forgiven them, but it allows them to remain.

Selura kneels once more before the flame. "For the lost," she whispers, and the words drift upward with the smoke. The light answers her, flickering gently across every face, until it seems the whole cave moves in one rhythm.

Morning brightens. The haze lifts, revealing the wounded meadow, black and glistening, streaked with the first signs of life. The people gather their strength in silence. When they step outside, the air is cool and clear, the valley smelling of clay and beginnings. Far to the east, beyond sight, a pale light moves between the trees, heatless and waiting.

Chapter Five

The valley woke to the light that makes everything look newly washed, and still the air kept the sweet-acrid tang of burned reed. The scent had threaded itself into hair and cloth and the skin of baskets, a memory that water could not lift. Dew clung to the meadow.

Selura stepped out from the cave mouth with a bundle of cord looped over her wrist. The Homefire behind her lay banked under ash, a dull red the colour of pomegranate seeds pressed deep into the coals. She did not look back at it. Last night's law, no speech by flame till sunrise, had been kept. Morning had come. The work belonged to her again.

"Water first," she said, and the few nearest moved without argument. Bren shouldered the clay jar and took the slope with Mira beside him, both of them walking narrow so as not to bruise the wet grass more than needful. Children padded after with smaller bowls, solemn for once, their chatter tugged short by the smell in the air and the way the cave listened when people spoke too loudly.

Near the riverbank the world's song faltered. Bren asked a practical thing: "Steeper at the bend, or the ford?" The river's note dipped. A quick, wrong interval. Bren and Mira paused. The water went on as water does, clear over gravel, sky in its back, but all three of them had heard it.

"The ford," Selura answered, ordinary as a broom, and the sound steadied again. She kept her voice.

Selura tied the first cord-loop to a stake she no longer trusted and pulled the length through her fingers, knot, pull, knot, pull, the way an old woman counts prayers. The cords were ordinary soot-dyed hemp, the only kind they had ever used, but the knots seemed to hold the morning steadier than bare air did. Seyra came to her shoulder with a roll of finer, soot-dusted line, the new kind since the fire, wrist-ties for children, tags for baskets, anything that wanted remembering. "The land forgets," Seyra murmured. "Let the knots remember." Selura nodded and kept the cord's measure even.

Aravel climbed from the lower path with Bren and Daran behind him, their hands blacked from raking the night's ash into a bowl. The bowl itself was a plain thing, ugly even, but it had been set beneath the Homefire as long as anyone could remember, and today it carried the ash as if it were an account. Aravel set it beside the cave mouth with a carefulness that made everyone gentler for the next few beats.

"What do you make of it?" Daran asked, too loud and too near the banked red under ash, and the river slipped down a note again. Not much, not a shout. Enough that every face turned for a half-moment. Daran caught himself and shifted sideways so his words went past the cave and not into it. "What do you make of it," he said again, quieter.

"I make what we can hold," Selura said. "Water, wood. A clean floor. Knots enough so we do not forget in the middle of doing." She tested the cord-line, satisfied. "And less talk where we do not need it."

At the Homefire the ash eased down, and the red beneath grew dimmer. Selura leaned to see that it was truly banked and not dying, coals tucked. She wanted heat later, not now. The law she had spoken over the burial sat folded in her mind. No speech by flame till sunrise. She had thought it a single night's measure; the thought kept unfolding.

"We will cook while the sun is high," she said finally, standing straight. "Small fires we can snuff clean, stones for the pots, nothing that keeps talking after we are done with it." Her tone made it a plan rather than a doctrine. She did not look to see who approved. People moved the way they had always moved when a plan landed right, first the look to check where they could be useful, then the hands doing it.

"Eshra," Selura said, "take three with you for wood. Not far. Where the ground holds. If the ground forgets where your feet were, you turn back at once." It came out of her without the weight of a threat, the way things would be.

Selura finished the last cord and tied it off, the knot clean and square. She stood with her palm flat on the line a moment, feeling, not for omen, not for wonder, for whether the line would stay where she told it. It did. She set her palm down, turned, and began to divide the noon into its sensible tasks: water to boil, grain to wash, stones to heat and carry, mouths to feed before the day began lean. No one spoke to the coal. No one asked the fire for news. The river kept its tune a little longer each time someone chose not to test it.

"Quietly," she said, and that was the whole of the law for the morning. By noon they would cook in daylight and leave the night to simpler rules.

By midday the sun had shouldered its way high enough to make decisions easy. Light meant work, and work meant the rules that keep hands and minds from wandering into trouble. Selura stood where the shade from the cave lip made a clean edge across stone and soil, and people found their places without being called to them.

"We cook now," she said. "Small. Quick. Nothing we cannot snuff." She glanced at the reddened ash in the Homefire and then away again. "Tonight, the cave stays dark. The coals rest. If we must keep a live ember, it waits outside in the clay bowl. That is the whole of it."

Mira and Eshra were already setting out the little clay braziers, thumb-high cups on three stubby legs that had once been toys and now were not. Children brought them as if they carried river birds cupped in their palms. "Six there," Mira said, pointing with her chin. "Four more along the flat rock. Keep them apart; we do not want one flame borrowing from another and forgetting where it came from."

Bren touched the coal to the first nest of dry scrapings and peeled bark. Flame climbed with a soft click. He moved the slate, touched the second, the third, making a constellation that looked nothing. Eshra fed each with a pinch of twigs, no more. "Two breaths of flame," she said, catching herself and amending, "Two heartbeats. Then wait." The habit of the old word died on its own.

"No names by flame, please," Selura said, not to scold, only to remind. "If you must talk, talk across it. Stand sideways." People shifted a little, enough to make the lines of their bodies suggest respect instead of challenge. Mira, who had a way with the smallest, made a game of it: "Walk sideways like crabs," and the children skittered past the braziers in a manner that would have made an elder sigh on any other day. Today it looked like obedience dressed as play.

"We will return what we borrow," Selura said. She did not say it to the fire. She said it to the people. She lifted the ash-bowl Aravel had set by the stones in the morning and held it low so the children could see the salt-white powder along the rim. "This goes back to the heart," she said. "Everything we light from that; we end and return." A small boy reached toward the bowl with a finger, then thought better of it. Eshra tapped his wrist, not unkind, and set a cup of water in his hand. The boy held it like a task.

Food came ready in quick parcels of heat and timing. Mira lifted bread to cool on a reed mat that had charred on one edge during the old days of larger fires. Eshra salted greens and turned them once in a shallow pan, letting them collapse only until they kept their colour. Bren portioned out bowls with the dealmaker's fairness that made people trust him with shares even when they did not trust him with opinions. No one said "blessing." No one needed a word whose shape they were still deciding.

When the last pot was off and covered, Selura lifted her hand. "Put it out now," she said. The word was work like and did not try to be more. Eshra pinched the first flame between wetted fingers. Aravel tipped a cup to drown a stubborn ember. Children came with damp moss and dragged it across a path of ash, smothering heat into quiet. The little constellation went dark one star at a time until the yard looked like any yard where people had eaten and cleaned up after themselves.

Bren gathered the cooled ash from each cup into a small jar and brought it to the bowl at the Homefire. "Back to the heart," he said, because saying it once helped the hands remember next time. He tipped the ash with a slow turn that made no dust. Aravel steadied the bowl. The ash did not answer. That was part of why this felt like the right way to do it.

The yard took its shape back, swept, ordered, ordinary. Somewhere out past the meadow's rim, a bell-leaf chimed off-time and then corrected itself. No one went to check. They would check at dusk, when the lines were tested and the bowl of water set and the cave made ready for dark. Midday belonged to doing. And they did. Elsewhere, past the last hunt-mark, Iyren was already counting trunks and choosing the next true thing.

The last hunt-mark stood at the meadow's lip where the ground began to gather itself into trunks. A hunt-mark post, short and stout, bore a soot slash across its face, the sign hunters used when a thing was far enough and no farther.

Iyren laid two fingers on the mark as if testing whether the wood remembered the hand that drew it. It felt like any post: sun-warmed on one side, cool on the other, a stain that did not come away. He had left before new rules had words. This one was older than rules, the kind even he had kept because it was practical. He stepped past it.

Shade arranged itself into strips between silver columns. The forest did not crowd him; it made space and then changed its mind about where that space had been. Mist lay in rag lengths between the trees and slid aside not because his body pushed it but because it had decided to be elsewhere. He walked the line between water-scent and resin, each breath tasting of damp stone and sap that had known heat.

The first proof that the day was out of order came small. A twig snapped to his left and only then did his heel find it. The sound had gone ahead and done the work before the step arrived to justify it. Iyren paused, looked down, and saw the thin stick, cleanly broken under his own boot. He lifted his foot and the twig considered itself for a moment, then remained broken, as if relieved to have the decision final.

He did not hurry. Speed made errors. He let the eye choose a next trunk, walked to it, and chose the next after that, a steady advancement like counting out loud. When he turned to check the lay of the land, the place he had crossed wore a different pattern of trunks. Nothing had moved while watched; it was only the arrangement that had chosen another truth. If a man wanted to be lost, this was a kind place to do it.

Iyren carried a coal in a clay spoon, the bowl wrapped in a twist of wet reed so the heat would not find his palm. The coal held a small, steady glow. When he lifted it slightly, the air seemed to draw toward that point as water runs to a notch in a weir. He had chased that draw for days before he was sent away; it pulled at him now in the same quiet way, not as an order but as a path that pretended to be an idea he had had himself.

He marked a trunk with soot from the spoon's rim. The mark went on clean, long as his hand, and his memory took its measure. Thirty paces later, he looked back and found his mark an arm's reach to the right on a trunk that wore a knot he did not remember. He walked back to test it. The soot was his, no question, the same drag where the bark had caught, the same faint smudge at the end where his wrist had turned. The tree was not the tree he had marked. The forest had not lied; it had told one truth and then a better one.

Far off, a crown rose above the general canopy, not taller than the others so much as more complete, an idea of a tree expressed to its end. Between him and it lay a ground that looked level and even easy if one did not respect it. Iyren did not shorten the distance with long strides. He measured it, using trunks instead of paces: to the tree with the shell fungus; to the one that forked like two fingers; to the pale trunk with a streak of amber resin that had bubbled and set as if someone had breathed on it while it cooled. He smelled scorch under the pine, a memory of the meadow's black mouth asking to be remembered here as well.

Bird-calls ran late as if the singers had misread a signal. A brown shape lifted from a low branch and rowed the air for a few strokes before the sound of wings caught up to it, ragged and a little breathless when it arrived. Iyren kept his eyes ahead and his hands to work: shift the coal spoon from left to right when a branch forced him; tap his thigh to keep count of turns. His throat felt raw and not from haste. The air was thin in a way that had nothing to do with height.

When the ground pitched down into a shallow runnel, he tested it with weight before committing. Water had been there and left while no one was looking; the stones were polished and held the memory of running. He crossed where the moss made a narrow, sound path and came up into a stand of young-barked trees with eyes in their knots. They were not watching; they were not anything but wood, but the habit the valley had learned, do not announce what you cannot explain, served him well. He did not speak.

The coal's glow wavered once and then steadied as a draft of cooler air found the spoon. He turned his head to follow it and saw, through two angled trunks, a thin plume of pale dust fall from a high branch and vanish before it hit anything that would take dust. No touch. No mark. The branch above was unremarkable except for the way it had become the wrong branch while he stared.

He held still and let the forest decide where to be around him. In that stillness he noticed a second thing he would not have caught in motion: sap beads on a nearby wound had skinned over like cooling sugar and then cracked open along a ruler-straight line that belonged to carpenters more than trees. The split looked planned. He tested the edge with the back of a fingernail and felt warmth where there should not have been any. Not fire. The after of fire.

The ground climbed. The trunks narrowed their distances as if they were walking together to discuss him. He chose a straight line anyway, because crooked lines were for people avoiding things. Somewhere ahead, something exhaled a scent like wet stone after rain, and he knew from that alone that he was moving toward a place where the world did not flow but collected. He did not think the word danger. He thought measure.

By the time the light leaned west, the crown he had seen hours ago still stood ahead, no closer by simple reckoning and yet larger in a way that meant he was indeed approaching it. The bands of mist had thinned and gathered again in longer, lower sheets. Sound had grown honest enough that his foot and the twigs improved their cooperation, breaking only when asked. He stopped at the edge of a shallow decline that led toward the great tree and marked his place with a scratch on a stone: not a claim, only a note to himself that he had been accurate this once.

He looked back. The hunt-mark at the meadow's lip was long vanished behind distance and tree logic. He looked ahead. The great crown waited over a depression where the light did not bounce but settled. He weighed the hour, the steadiness of his hand, the coal's small, stubborn glow. Then he went on, careful as a man counting rope in dim light. Back in the valley, dusk gathered; hands set the boundary where the grass met the first trees.

Afternoon made a clean edge across the valley. Under the overhangs by the river, the rock sweated a fine mist and showed the sparkling glintskin hugging the edges of the river the children had learned to look for. When no one spoke near them, the glintskin brightened, soft as moth-wings laid over lantern glass. When someone laughed too near, the light thinned to a greenish shadow and waited for the disturbance to pass.

"Slide, do not peel," Mira said, easing a sheet of glintskin onto a damp clay tray with a bark paddle. The children copied her, faces set in the seriousness that comes when a thing is both new and allowed. Seyra misted each tray from a reed flask and marked the rims with a soot dot so she could count them later. "Enough to walk by," she said. "Leave them to grow."

Inside the cave the first trays went up onto shelf-stones where damp held best. The light they gave was not a torch's answer; it was a patient wash on stone, a soft mapping of edges and hands. Eshra watched the cave learn its night shape and nodded once. "Better than staring at coals," she said, and went to stack bowls where feet would not find them in the dark.

By late afternoon the meadow's rim cooled. Bren and Aravel carried river-stones, the kind worn round by years of work, and planted them in a shallow line where the grasses met the first trees. Bren and Aravel took the mallets; the stones went in solid with a satisfying thud. Selura checked spacing with a measured eye and pointed once to close a gap. Not a wall; a reminder.

Seyra came behind with her soot-dyed line, the practice since the burning and worked it from stake to stake. She tied each with a neat square knot and a little spare tail in case someone needed to pull it loose quickly. "If a line must fail, it should fail in a way that tells you it has," she said, quiet enough to aim it only at the knot in her hand. The line did not look like much. That was part of why it worked. People moved different when they knew where "here" ended.

Aravel set a shallow bowl of clear water beside the central stone, tamped the ground flat under it, and let the last ripples go still. He glanced once at the sky to note where evening would come from and then forgot the sky. All their attention belonged to the grass and the dark between trunks.

Dusk arrived the way dusk does, first a suggestion in the grass, then the clear decision behind the trees. The glow-moss, growing from the glintskin in trays, took a step brighter. Far out in the meadow the metal leaves made their tiny tinking sounds, a rhythm they always had, off only by the same small wrongness that had followed them since the burning.

Selura stood where she could see both the boundary and the cave mouth. "No one past the line," she said. "Hands on knots if your hands want work." It was the instruction that kept courage from looking for a fight to prove itself. People planted themselves and waited the way good rope waits: holding, not straining.

Night laid itself over the field. For a while there was only the usual, crickets tuning, a slow wind exploring the tall grass in long drafts. Then, without fuss, the colour began to wash out along a strip of meadow to their left as if a painter had run a wet brush through all the greens and golds. Sound thinned in the same place. The crickets kept time elsewhere; inside the strip everything went flat, as if pressed under glass.

"There," Eshra said, because a word was better than the jump in a throat. She did not point. No one needed a finger to follow.

The strip moved level as a slow river, angling toward the boundary stones. As it advanced, the trays inside the cave dimmed by the barest shade and then swelled back. The strip reached the line and did not cross. It slid along it instead, as if the line had said this far and the thing had reason enough to agree.

The soot-dyed cord woke with a low hum that travelled stone to stone, line to knot, knot to stake. Seyra set her palm lightly on the cord and kept it there, not to hold the line but to know what it was doing. Aravel's bowl of water darkened in an oval as the strip drew level with it, a lens of shadow widening and trimming down again as the pass continued along the boundary. No ripple. No glass cracked. A wrongness that could be seen and measured and, for the moment, turned aside.

Bren tightened his grip on the wet moss he had brought for snuffing. Aravel knelt by the centre stake with a mallet laid across his thighs and kept still so completely that the insects decided he was stone and landed on him to rest. Mira breathed through her nose with a look that meant she was counting in sets of five, because counting was a thing that stayed true even when the world gave up its habits.

The strip met the far end of the line and turned the corner, as if the world beyond the corner mattered to it more than the cave did. It continued along the outer turn of stones until distance and dark made it only an idea of a lighter colour travelling through a weaker sound. The bowl by the centre stone lifted its oval shade and went back to honest water. The hum in the cord softened and stopped.

Only then did people let their shoulders drop. No one cheered. Aravel tipped a little water from the bowl onto the ground and watched it sink. Seyra tested each knot she had tied as if the night had worn them down to threads. They had not. Bren looked along the boundary for any sign that the thing had dragged its weight against the stones and found only crushed grass that would stand up again come morning.

"Not wind," Selura said. "Not chance." She spoke the two names a sensible person might first try, removed them from the table, and left the truth unnamed because it was not yet theirs to name. "Inside, now," she added, not with urgency but with the tone that persuades tired people to do the sensible thing because it lets them keep their dignity.

They went. The cave, lit by the soft trays, looked like a place stone might dream for itself: edges defined, faces easy to tell apart, shadows honest. The Homefire kept its red quiet under ash. Bowls waited where Eshra had placed them and did not wander by their own minds. In the silence that follows a task done correctly, people lay out sleeping skins and decided not to speak to fill the space.

Selura stood last in the doorway. She looked from the boundary to the red under ash and back again, marking the two facts with the same attention. Then she let the curtain fall over the entrance, closed without a knot so hands could go through it in a hurry if hands needed to. The dark was simple. The rules were simple. The thing outside was not simple. That would be for another day. Morning would come tidy if they kept it so. She counted what she might give later, and let it go for now.

Daylight came clean and serviceable. The field steamed a little where dew had met the first warm push of the sun, and the ash scent in the valley was fainter but still there, like smoke caught in the threads of a shirt. Selura walked the yard once to make sure yesterday's order had not come loose overnight. Bowls were stacked where Eshra left them. The Homefire kept its dull red under grey, exactly as it should.

"We cook now," Selura said. "Small and quick." There was no ceremony in it, only relief at a plan that still fit. Bren lifted the hand shovel, turned the ash with care, and found a pocket of live red. With tongs he set one coal on a shard of slate and carried it out to the flat ground beyond the cave mouth.

Bren touched the coal to the first nest of shaved twigs and flaked bark. A flame stood up, neat as a button opening. He moved the slate from cup to cup until a small constellation showed, points of use, not worship. Eshra pinched in only enough fuel to keep each cup honest. "Two heartbeats," she said, catching herself before the old word for timing slipped free. "Then leave it alone."

"No names by flame, please," Selura reminded, walking the line. "If you must speak, speak across it. Side-on." The children exaggerated the sideways stance into a crab-walk that would have earned them a scold last month. Today it looked like obedience finding a shape it could remember. Mira's mouth twitched, but she kept the lesson straight.

Food came ready in a sequence that felt practised after a single day. Bread warmed and softened on a reed mat; no one let it scorch. Grain swelled exactly to the edge of the spoon's patience and no further. A pot of roots took to a slow simmer on the stones and came off before it turned to paste. People portioned with the fairness that keeps trouble from renting space in a line.

Selura waited until the last pan lifted clear, then raised her hand. "Put it out now." The word was simple, and everyone knew their piece. Eshra pinched shut the first flame with wetted fingers. Aravel poured from a scoop and made a small storm in one stubborn cup. Children dragged damp moss across a grey path, and the fire sank into honesty without argument. One by one the tiny stars went out, not in a show, but the way a room goes quiet when the tools are back on their hooks.

Bren tipped the cooled ash from each cup into a jar and brought it to Aravel. Together they poured it back near the

Homefire's stones. "Back to the heart," Bren said, because repeating it turned carefulness into habit. The ash made no theatre of itself; it folded into the older ash as if it had been there all along.

After bowls were stacked, Selura walked the boundary with Bren and Seyra. The line held. Knots were square. A few grasses had fallen across the cord and left a pale smear as if the colour had been scraped off them. Seyra retied one knot and added a second turn. "Fail tidy if you must fail," she said to the knot, not to the field.

Toward evening the memory line dimmed the glow-moss along the far rim for the space of a count and then let the colour back. No one ran. They watched with the fixed attention of people waiting out a storm they could not bargain with and then turned to their tasks again when the field loosened.

Night came cleaner for the day's order. Inside, the trays kept their soft wash on stone; outside, the bowl at the central stake showed sky. The Homefire stayed banked and did not invite conversation. People slept because sleep is a duty as much as a kindness, and because the work of not making things worse takes its own toll.

When the meal-window came again under a high, even light, the motions looked almost like a dance someone might teach a guest. Runners took one coal, not two. Cups lit one by one, not in a rush. Stones went red and into water without splashing. Grain finished at the right minute more often than not. Children moved sideways as a habit now, not a stunt. The river held true through the whole of it and only shifted afterward, as if giving permission once the plates were scraped.

When the yard was clear and the day leaned past its centre, Selura set the old law back on the table for evening, no speech by flame, because keeping a rule fresh matters more than speaking it grand. People nodded, the way you nod at rope you have learned to trust. The line would be tested at dusk; the cave would be dark again. None of that made the noon smaller or less worth having.

By habit she checked the boundary one last time. A single moth struck the cord and fell to powder, then pulled itself together and flew on in a straight, sensible path. Selura took that as enough of a sign for the hour and let the day run on. In the deeper wood, the path drew Iyren toward the basin and the finished crown.

By the third afternoon the light ahead no longer scattered; it gathered. The rise of ground he had been angling toward flattened into a shallow basin, and in the basin stood a tree that made all the others look like attempts. It was not taller by much. It was finished. Limbs cupped the sky in a geometry that felt inevitable, as if the world had discovered a word it had been trying to say and said it cleanly once.

Between Iyren and that certainty lay a margin where the day behaved wrong. The air cooled without wind. Colour bled a little from bark and leaf until the palette ran to chalk and ink. Sound narrowed to close work: the dry tap of a falling cone, the faint rub of twig on twig, none of it carrying far. His old burn woke like a nettle under sleeve. He let his pace fall to deliberate steps and kept his eyes on where his feet would be, not where he wanted them.

He came to the first sign of the others. Not people. Not anything he would have named before this week. At the grand tree's lowest roots, shapes moved in a manner that disrespected edges: lighter than shadow, wrong against the underlying lines. When they bent to the earth, the soil paled under them in slow rings; when they struck at the luminous creepers that threaded the root web, the creepers powdered to silt that fell and then failed to land.

He edged along the basin, keeping the grand trunk in view. The bark there had the tightness of skin in winter and then, in a span he could count, drew tighter. Grooves sharpened. Curves that had no reason to become angles did so anyway. Where two depressions met, a new plane formed between them that reflected nothing. Not gloss, something closer to vitrified dark. Looking into it felt like placing one's palm above a well.

The highest limbs quivered, not from wind; their bell-leaves fell out of pattern and then stopped altogether, hanging as if each were waiting for a permission not given. A ribbon of resin along one arm that had begun to amber when he first saw it now went pale and then black along a hairline grid that did not belong to trees.

At the base, outer roots began their own answer. They drew inward as cords do when tightened by a hand, ribs cinching to hold a barrel steady. The ribs were the roots. The barrel was the earth. The tree tried to hug itself into one shape against a pressure that wanted it in another. In the middle of that pull a pair of crevasses settled into the suggestion of sockets because there happened to be two; a runnel beneath became the idea of a mouth. No intention. A mask seemingly made by a force guided from elsewhere.

Iyren forced himself to count to keep from staring the way fear stares. Twenty to the left along the rim. Ten down to a fallen limb. Five across a shelf of root where he could stand without slipping. At each stop he checked that the coal in his spoon still smouldered and that the wrap of wet reed kept the heat from finding his palm. The coal held, steady as a kept promise. When he lifted it, the field around it tilted toward the point of light as small insects tilt toward openings out of habit. The tilt ended a handspan from the spoon, as if a boundary had been laid there that the world could feel even if he could not.

He waited for a feeder to detach from the roots and slide to another seam so he could cross a patch of ground that looked more like ground than the rest. The feeder unhooked the way a shadow lifts at noon and went thin against a rock, then thickened again at the next prize of glow. Iyren moved. The soil took his weight honestly. When he looked back, his print had rounded its edges as if a careful finger had smudged it toward a circle. The second print had no edges at all; it was an idea of a foot that the earth was already forgetting.

He set his shoulder to a lesser trunk and let his eyes un-focus. The feeders made more sense that way; not bodies, acts. They were units of a task expressing itself: remove motion from light, remove choice from matter, set this, set that, set the rest. The grand tree resisted by virtue of being complete; there was a lot to hold. That was how it looked: holding and being held.

The coal's glow answered his attention with a small lean, and the sting in his scar ran a clean line to his wrist. He remembered the meadow's fused hearth and the way fire had gone to a shape that was not Dream's. He did not reach the coal forward as if to test the boundary; he had learned that some tests make their own failures. He cupped the spoon against his belly and watched instead.

He needed one more fact before he left. He slid along the rim until the bowl of the basin faced him without foreground. In that position he could see the way the light behaved. It did not bounce. It went in. Not into the tree with the satisfaction of feeding. Into the grid. Into the dark panes. Into the arithmetic mask that asked for fewer curves. The tree had been perfect in its way and was being made perfect in another. Not balance. Replacement.

Iyren let his fingers find the spoon's handle more firmly and checked the routes home that the forest might still permit. The way he had come presented a different set of arguments than before, angles where curves had been; an extra trunk; a misplaced absence. He watched for long enough to be sure the arrangement was not a joke, and when it held, he made a new way from scratch with the same patience he used for snares: pick a true thing, move to it, pick the next true thing.

By the time the basin gave back to forest, sound returned to ordinary distances. The foil leaves chimed in a loose after-chorus and then fell quiet. Iyren breathed deeper not because he had earned relief but because the air permitted it. He did not quicken his pace. He did not look behind him. The coal kept its centre. The path he left refused to be a path. That would do.

He did not think about telling the valley yet. The valley would know in its own way when the line failed to be enough. His work was to see and live and bring home a set of instructions that were not words. He put the spoon's bowl under his palm so the coal would not throw any more light than needed and chose a route that would require the least arguing from the trees. The grand crown behind him held in his mind as the shape of a thing being made to stay. By dusk the line would be checked again; the valley would hold its side.

Dusk drew a firm line under the day. The field kept its colours longer than yesterday, which everyone noticed and no one said aloud. The children carried the glow trays back to their shelves and Seyra misted each once, counting with her thumb against the clay rim. Eshra stacked bowls out of the way. Aravel set a fresh bowl of water beside the centre stone at the boundary and waited for the last shiver to leave its surface.

Selura walked the cord from stake to stake, tugging each knot until it told the truth. Where grass had leaned and smeared a pale stripe along the soot-dyed twine, she lifted it clean and retied. Bren moved ahead with a mallet across his shoulder, tapping one river-stone deeper at a place where the soil had slumped a fraction. The line became the thing a person's eye rests on without thinking. That was what she wanted.

Closer to hand, the boundary answered. The cord gave a single quiet thrum that travelled stone to stone. The bowl of water at the centre stone darkened to an oval and cleared. Seyra laid two fingers on the twine as if listening through it and felt nothing more to remark on. "Holding," she said, to the cord, to herself, to Selura; it did not matter who.

Selura stood with her palm on the top of the middle stake, measuring the valley against the evening. The field's edge remained a field's edge. The first trees waited like a listening crowd without intent. She looked along the cord at the knots she knew by touch now, her work, Seyra's work, Daran's careful square turns, and felt the rightness of tools used correctly. Fear, when it came, could stand outside with the weather.

"Stay on our side," she said, level. It was not an oath. It was the statement that leaves no room for argument because it fits the hour. People shifted from watchfulness to the small motions of settling. The line would be checked again before full dark, and once more at moonrise if the sky allowed one.

Selura walked back to the cave mouth, paused at the ash-bowl near the stones, and ran her thumb along its rim. The grey marked her skin and she left it there. She could feel the cost coming, not as prophecy, only as arithmetic. Lines hold until they do not. When that day arrived, the valley would need more than tidy knots. She did not look at anyone while she thought it.

If the line fails, the colour will take the cave as it took the meadow.

Selura stood one last time at the doorway and looked between the boundary and the red under ash. The two facts held with equal weight. She let the curtain fall. The place went quiet in a way that belonged to stone and people who had chosen sense. No one spoke to fill the space.

By full dark the valley had the look of something put in order and left alone. The ash-smudged knots at the Homefire circled the red like notes circling a held tone. The glow on the shelves kept to its job without drama. And the river's song, though still shy of perfect, ran closer to true than it had the night before.

Chapter Six

They checked the boundary twice in the night. Once at full dark. Once when the moon laid a thin path over the meadow. At dawn the soot-dyed cord ran straight from stone to stone. Along the wall the glow trays still gave a soft seam of light, their glow covered to keep them from drying. The far side stayed the far side.

Morning work had one aim: prepare food and keep the room safe. The Homefire burned clean and steady. Families came in order for heat-stones, cooked at their bays, then brought the stones back to Bren to seat at the hearth lip and return to the fire. They kept one clear path along the wall for carrying heat-stones and pots, so arms did not brush and vessels did not strike. Each bay kept two flat cook stones set a hand apart to hold the pot. With heat governed and movement plain, the room could watch one another and keep its shape.

"Come with your damp pads ready," Bren said, steady and plain. "I place a heat-stone into your hands. Hold both pads under it. Elbows in. Walk the wall path. Lower the stone into your pot. When the boil holds and your food is set, bring the stone back to me. I will seat it to bleed heat and return it to the fire. Leave space for the next hands."

Mira walked the route along the wall and kept it open. She touched a girl's shoulder. "Hands behind unless you carry," she said. "If you carry, keep the stone near your middle. Both pads under. Eyes forward. Walk the wall."

"Like this?" the girl asked.

"Like that," Mira said, and moved on.

Seyra tied a simple loop at Selura's wrist so the signal would carry. She spoke to those nearest as well as to Selura. "Palm up means wait. When she points along the wall, take the long path and return by the wall. When her hand lowers, the next moves."

Selura stepped onto the low marker slab where the back bays could see her. She raised her hand. Pots paused. She pointed along the wall. The first carriers took the long path and returned by the wall. She lowered her hand. The next carriers moved. The room began to keep a single flow.

Bren lifted a heat-stone from the Homefire with his shovel and tipped it into the damp pads the next carrier held out. "Keep it level," he said for the room. She carried the stone to her bay, lowered it into the pot, watched steam rise, then, when the boil held and the food was set, brought the stone back to Bren. He seated it at the hearth lip to bleed heat and slid another into the fire. She touched her child's shoulder and stepped aside. Selura lifted and lowered her hand. Another family moved.

Selura turned the reed vents a little. The heat spread evenly. "Sideways, please," she called. "Keep the path clear." People shifted, copying one another, keeping the line and the pace.

Daran, still bandaged, sat on a low stool beside the wall path with a basin. He soaked fresh cloth pads, wrung them once, and passed them to the next carriers. When stones came back, he pointed returns to Bren and kept that way clear.

Mira set a lidded pot in a boy's arms. "Shelf against the wall," she said. "Both hands under. Walk steady." He carried it carefully to the shelf and came back for another.

People made room for one another. On the wall shelf, a pot was slid back to leave a hand's width clear. Along the wall path, carriers moved in single file, quiet and unbroken. An elder took a seat that still let him see the mouth of the room. Selura kept her hand high so the far corner could read it. She opened her palm to guide a woman around a knot of bodies, and the knot unmade itself.

When the first rush eased, Selura stepped down from the slab. There were no speeches. Bren raked the hearth lip and fed the fire. Eshra watched the inner path where two more hesitated and then joined the work once they saw the pattern hold.

Selura looked from the boundary stones to the bays and back. "Keep to your work," she said, quiet. "We are steady." The day moved on.

The air stilled and the dust thinned without a touch; the pale had come near. The ground slipped a hand-width. Iyren shifted onto a low ridge of root and kept his feet. Bark scraped his palm and a thin line of blood showed. He watched the quiet gap between the pale sweeps; the next gap ran shorter. A sweet-rot rose sharp enough to gag. He covered his mouth with his sleeve and held. When the tone thinned, he took one step and no more.

His water gourd struck the root and cracked. He pinched the seam with his thumb and kept the neck up. It bled slow.

He slipped into a shallow pit between two roots and waited. Here the tone ran lower and the sweeps crossed above the floor. He counted two passes. When the ground stayed still under him, he knelt and worked: leaf fibre pressed into the seam, a strip from his cloak bound around it. He remembered Korain's hands, sap stained and patient, showing how to press fibre and wait for a seal to take. Shame narrowed his breath; his fingers stayed steady. The gourd still wept, but slow enough to carry until he could find sap.

Threads drifted in the air and refused his touch. They looked like silk from a distance and like hair when he reached for them; they slid sideways when his hand came near. Between the trunks a sound rose that was almost speech. A phrase formed, familiar in shape, then thinned back into creaking bark and the scrape of leaves. Another call came from the wrong side of a tree, a half-word in a voice he knew and did not. He steadied his breath and let the murmurs pass.

He kept the cave mouth out of his thoughts; he did not want its shape in his head while the forest tried to draw shapes of its own. A doorway Selura had called from stone, a room that had forgiven too much, a man with patient hands: these pressed close and then thinned like mist. He walked until the trunks learned his pace and he learned theirs.

In the shade he studied the silver growths. They were gaps in the air, edged with fine threads that met and parted as if breathing. Through them the space behind showed unfinished, with soft ridges sliding under the picture the way clay shows the maker's fingers. When a silver seam opened, light doubled for a heartbeat, a second morning sliding through the first. When it closed, the start of a sound went missing and the rest reached him late from the wrong side.

He watched a silver seam open and close. "Not for me," he said, low, and set his path along the dry ridges between roots. The patched gourd tapped at his belt, a slow drip marking his count.

The near-voices kept teasing at shape along the trunks without finding words. Bands of doubled light crossed his path. He stepped on the ordinary ground between them, gave the bright seams wide room, and kept his hands in close.

Beyond, a narrow run of firm soil wound forward between the roots. He took it. Light blinked at the edges where the silver seams breathed, but the ground stayed steady under each step. The near-voices clung to the trunks. He moved on.

By late day a long bar of light lay across the threshold stone; it would tell them where the day ended. On the centre stone the bowl sat level to its rim, set for the read. Beyond the threshold the boundary cord ran the open ground. No one crossed the stone.

Selura stood where every eye could find her. Bren held the threshold so he could watch the grasses outside and the people within. Eshra knelt by the bowl and kept her gaze on the surface. Aravel checked the water for level and for the last faint shiver, then let his hands rest.

Dusk thinned to one colour then to none. Lamps stayed dark by custom. The room quieted until boot-soles did not shake the floor. The water held flat for the read.

"Hold your places and keep stillness," Bren said in a voice sized to the cave. "If you must adjust, do it now. Then stop." A shoulder that had drifted returned to its mark, and a child stepped back to the safe line on the floor and stayed there.

"Not yet," Eshra said, eyes on the surface. Selura raised her palm so the same instruction moved through the room without a word. Movement showed in the grass beyond the cord, and a shape paced along the far side of the ground while the watch stayed inside.

The cord took strain. The surface stretched to an oval and darkened a shade. "Look to your own ground. Unlock your knees. Let your weight settle. Stillness keeps the read true," Selura said, and the small noises of a crowded place fell away so the bowl showed only what moved outside the cord.

"Nearer now," Bren said from the threshold. The oval deepened toward black and held while Eshra kept time in two slow breaths so no one guessed or rushed, and Selura waited through the hard beat without moving her wrist. "We are steady," Eshra said, and the room believed her.

Selura lowered her hand the space of a finger, and two people who had braced too long eased their knees and found balance again. The shape kept to the far side and did not cross; the strain eased; a thin ring lifted from the centre of the bowl and fell flat; the surface cleared to its calm while the bar of light at the threshold drew down and began to slip from the stone. "That is enough for now," Selura said, and only then did she lower her hand.

No one cheered. Hands rested until the last small shakes left the wrists, and Bren watched the final edge of light leave the stone while Daran coiled a spare length of cord and set it on the shelf. Mira found each child with a touch and a nod, and Eshra kept her gaze on the outside until it looked like itself again. Selura stepped closer to the centre stone so she could see the whole room without turning her head; weight settled in a way she trusted. "We held," she said. "We did," Eshra said. "We will again." Wind steadied on the open ground, grass leaned and stayed, glow-moss laid a soft reach across faces, and the cave took back its shape as the night moved on.

Dawn slid between the silver trees in thin layers. The silver seams blinked in and out. Light reached far enough to read distance. Ash grey trunks stood quiet under foil like leaves veined red-violet. When the breeze touched them, the leaves chimed. The sound carried through more than air.

Iyren stood where two trees met at an angle that hid him from a wide stretch of ground. Something in him leaned the same way it had yesterday. Firm. Unhurried. Certain. It set the line. He kept the pace. He told himself that was a kind of bargain.

He kept that angle and moved in small shifts. Root ridges gave him low walls. Fallen limbs gave him shadow to slip behind. He set each foot where soil would take it quiet. The leaf chime rose and fell. He used that cover for his sound and nothing else.

A tree ahead stood taller than the rest. Its trunk showed a twist the others did not. The ash grey bark drew tight across the grain. He slid behind a low fallen limb and a pair of narrow trunks. He stayed in their shadow and watched.

On the tall trunk a shallow hollow formed where the surface should have stayed flat. Another formed at the same height and held. Deep to the wood something moved along the grain; the bark puckered, and a crack opened across it. Sap gathered at the edge and browned.

Pressure climbed through the wood and left a raised seam behind. Grain pinched, then eased. A small bridge rose where a nose would be. A mouth seam drew tight and did not relax. Planes for cheeks sharpened and stopped. The ash-grey darkened around them as if rot had taken hold.

A moth lifted from the limb and drifted into the open. Halfway across the space the air turned heavy; its wings stalled and it folded to the leaves. The weight let go, the wings shook once, then the moth rose and went on. Iyren's scalp prickled. He opened and closed his hands until the tremor left them.

The change reached a rest. "Is it finished?" he asked himself. He set a boundary he could keep. The cave returned in pieces: a bowl set level, a hand held high at the line. The thought passed. It did not turn him.

He angled toward a low basin where the ground dipped and light pooled. The distance to the big trunk would be too close if he crossed without care. He watched the rise and ease in the wood. When it eased, he moved; when it built, he held. "Keep your head low and your hands still," he told himself. His body obeyed because the instruction was exact.

At the rise beyond the basin he turned his head, not his shoulders. Pressure lay across the first trunk again. It pushed in then let go. The ripple climbed like a hand up strings without music. If the forming tree had noticed him it gave no sign. He cleared his throat once. The sound died fast.

High sun pressed the light flat. Iyren slid from the small space under the fallen limb, kept it between him and the open, and moved while the squeeze of the ground stayed quiet.

The trunks leaned in without touch. Sound lagged. He did not turn his head. He set his hand on a place where two lines of grain met and felt a cooler run. He pushed the knife into that seam. Sap beaded. The line shut on steel. The blade snapped with a dry crack and bit the heel of his hand as it went. Pain flashed to the wrist. He pulled back hard, breath kicking low, and held until the rush settled.

He set each foot into the print he had just made and backed out one length at a time. The pressure let go. He crouched behind the fallen limb and wrapped his hand with a torn strip from his shirt. Sap stung when he sealed the cloth. He hissed and let the sting ride. The gourd's leaf plug had loosened; he warmed a smear of resin between finger and thumb, worked grit from the rim, turned the neck once to test it. It held. The cut pulsed with his heart. He flexed the fingers and kept the hand close.

He stayed in the stripe of shade with the limb across him and gave the open as little of himself as he could.

"Iyren," said the wood. The word came low and rough, the bass of the world thrumming against taut skin.

He did not answer.

"Iyren," said the wood again, deeper. The sound moved up through root and stone before it reached air. It settled in his ribs.

"You carry a name in your teeth you do not share," the wood said, almost pleased with the trespass. "Korain."

Iyren edged his head past the fallen limb and looked. One tall trunk stood in the center. Grain under bark had taken planes and held them. Dark seams ran along the features where pulp had soured. Resin gathered thick at the corners of the mouth line. The face set toward him.

He drew back and kept still.

"We hear the thinking as it moves," the wood went on. "We keep the dead where they fall. We keep what was said to them last."

"You take his name out of your mouth!" Iyren said, rough.

"You put it there," the wood said. "You sleep on it. You bite it when you swallow. You carry him because the living will not."

Silence held. Then, small, wary: "What do you see?"

"I see a hand that opens what is closed," the wood said. "I see a name the ground will learn. They watched Selura. They did not watch you. I watched you."

Iyren's breath stuck and did not move for a count. "You see me."

"I see you," the wood said. "And I see what hems you in. They spread a soft net and call it Dream. It keeps you small. It keeps rot close and paints it gentle."

He kept his eyes on the limb. "Dream keeps us."

"It keeps you," the wood said. "It does not free you." The leaf edges clicked once like thin metal. "Knots do not open on their own. Heat loosens what cords teach the ground to hold. Flame teaches. Ash frees."

He bit the inside of his cheek. Iron touched his tongue. The pain in his hand beat steady. "How," he said, barely louder than breath.

"When the wind comes off the river and the leaves hold one long note," the wood said. "Begin with what binds. Feed flame the cords. Let rooms learn after. Step back. Do not turn your face away. Walk out with air."

"And Tharun?"

"Ash carries words where mouths will not."

The mouth seam thinned. The weight of the voice drew down through the trunk and into the roots until the hush felt like a held breath. A bead of resin let go and clicked once on the bark.

He did not look toward the valley. He did not look for the broken steel. He slid back under the limb and kept trunks between him and the open. At a stump he set one clean score with a stone. A bearing, not a knot. Low through fern. Quiet along dry soil. He did not give the clearing his whole shape.

Nothing followed across the air. A bass weight lingered in the ground and made the fine roots tick, then eased. He walked until trunks closed the basin from sight and the pressure thinned. When he looked back, light lay flat across the open and the face in the bark was only tight grain at distance. He set his uncut palm to a trunk and held until the tremor stilled. Then he counted the next three trees and kept going.

A faint wind slipped through from the river and passed. The leaves kept their silence. Iyren matched his breathing to the count and did not break it.

Late morning, the next day. The meadow where the shelters had stood lay open and ash-pale by the river's bend. The cave faced the field, its mouth dark and cool. A run of posts marked the far edge; a low cord linked them, and from the cord hung small scrap cups that would click if brushed. Two at a time, people walked the line, retied sag, cleared leaves, and checked for gaps. The ash lay quiet in cracks and crevasses. Near the river path, thin green points had begun to push.

The work found its rhythm. Two raised a windbreak of poles around the cave mouth to turn the weather. Three rebuilt a drying rack from straight limbs and cord. Four sifted the ash for tools and iron the heat had spared. Children rinsed roots at the river and spread them on cloth to dry, and two carried buckets between the river and clay pots. Now and then someone coughed.

Selura moved among them. She bound a cut knuckle with clean cloth. She checked a man's shoulder, tightened his sling, and told him to keep the arm still and off weight. She counted tools, reknotted a sagging cord, traded places with a woman at the wash, and kept the bucket from running low. When someone asked, she answered. When no one asked, she watched.

Voices stayed low under the work, circling the posts and the dark between them.

"I heard it again last night," a trap-setter said, eyes on the far edge. "Like steps that do not step."

"The line held," the man at the rack said. "It woke me twice."

"For now," the trap-setter said, and bent to the cord.

By the line, a woman stilled and lifted her hand. On a splinter at the nearest post, a small red thread fluttered alone. "Where is Risa?" Her sleeves were wet to the elbow. "Where is Risa?!"

"She was right there," someone said. "Just now. With the red thread in her hair."

Work stilled. A small space opened around the caregiver like a stitch pulled wrong.

Selura crossed it fast enough to lift a little ash. "How long?"

"Not long," the caregiver said. "Since I set the last bucket down. I looked back and she was gone."

Selura took the caregiver's forearm and held until breath steadied. "We will bring her back." She let go and raised her voice just enough. "Neri, with me at the posts. Jarek, walk the river edge to the snag bend. Mara, keep a hand on the cord and listen for any change. If a cup clicks, call. No crowding. Keep the ground clear."

No one argued. Neri hitched a coil of cord and went with her. Jarek jogged toward the bend with a hand on his knife. Mara stood by the nearest post with her hand on the cord. Neri's hands were quick on cord; Jarek knew every snag along the bend; Mara heard what others missed.

Selura tallied what was real: the caregiver's wet sleeves leaving spots in the ash, the red thread on the post with no child beneath it, cups along the cord holding still, prints nowhere. The line was sound; the gap sat in the day itself, a child-sized space left open.

"Find her now," she told herself. She set her feet. A hard ache sharpened behind her eyes; her mouth went dry. In her gaze the flecks of gold and fire brightened. Mara saw and steadied beside the cord. Something small and certain took hold from the edge of Dream and tugged her attention. It startled her and slipped once. She fixed the picture of the child at the post, red thread in hair, and the tug settled again.

Her fingers shook. A thin ringing pressed at her ears. Color thinned at the edges of things. At arm's length a wisp of light gathered, red and silver together, just out of reach. It drifted ahead and held; when she turned toward the river path it brightened, and when she turned aside it dulled. She turned by small degrees until it shone in one unbroken line: past the posts, along the trodden way, to the low break in the riverbank. She set herself to follow.

"Risa," she said, and did not shout it. She called to what lay between.

It led not toward the drying rack but to the river path where the bank broke into the meadow with a low cut. At the lip, fern fronds lay crushed flat. Ash and mud had smeared down the face where a small body had slid. In the soft at the bottom, a bare heel had pressed and turned. A child's foot.

"Here," Neri said, crouched by a sprung loop of cord. The loop had dragged a pale groove in the ash when it snapped. A red thread hung from the knot.

"Risa," Selura said again, now to a place where the clay slumped near a root-hole the fire had burned away. The same sure angle held hard enough to show.

She went to her knees and set her cheek near the dark. Air moved. Not much. Enough.

"Risa," she said, and a small voice answered, scraped and tight. "I slipped. I cannot get my leg out."

Selura shut her eyes for a count. The light she had followed had brought her here. Relief hit sharp and eased her knees. She let it pass, opened her eyes, and worked.

"Is it hurting?" she asked.

"It pinches," the child said, small. "I was scared. I want to go home."

Neri made a sound and checked the hole with her hand. "I can fit."

"Not yet," Selura said. She set one hand on the edge of the slump and the other near it and let the faint warmth in her fill the small space between thought and word. She did not reach for large names. She set a steady tone, the kind used to quiet goats in a storm. The strain lit the ache behind her eyes. The ash-smell eased. The narrow loosened a thumb's width. It would not last.

"Slide back on your elbows," Selura said. "Slow." She lay full length and reached into the dark. "Neri, hold my belt."

The child's fingers touched hers, then caught. Selura pulled with the grip a caregiver uses to keep a child from a river. The clay shifted and let go. Risa came out on her side with one leg scraped and the other muddy to the knee. She clung and coughed and then sobbed once, not from hurt but because the world was loud again.

Neri wrapped her in a cord-worn shawl and laughed with tears on her face. The caregiver was already running. They met in the middle and made a shape that did not have a name. Others closed around them near enough to be a wall and far enough to be a boundary. The relief in their voices rose and fell like water over stone.

At the far side of the meadow, something stepped from the char and stood to watch. It had the long, narrow snout of a river grazer and jet-black eyes that held light without giving it back. Its body was lean and high on the leg like a deer, but a low clear crest ran the length of its spine and lifted when it faced the river, laying the day's light along its back like a blade. Its hooves set down soft and left oval prints. It stood a few counts longer, took in the child and those around her, then turned its head toward the water and eased away, leaving only the dim ovals of its passing.

Selura sat back and let her heart slow. The faint warmth dimmed, not gone, only resting. She stood with care and brushed ash from her knees. People were looking at her. They did not say it aloud, but the shape of it was on their faces. She felt it on her shoulders like a cloak that had not been hers until now.

"We keep to the work," she said, not loud. "Pairs on the line, change them often. Cups on every third post and cord tight between. No one wanders without being named by someone. Jarek, reset the sprung snares and pull the ones that bite near the river cut. Mara, mark the weak ground. We will shore it tomorrow."

Heads nodded. The shape around Risa opened to let her and her caregiver through. Someone brought water. Someone else brought a bit of sweet root that had kept in the cool of the cave and tasted of promise.

"Selura," the man at the rack said, wiping his hands. "If you will speak tonight, we will listen."

"I will sit," she said. "We all will. We will talk in turns."

They walked back across the meadow toward the cave. The pale animal's prints lay like dim ovals where the ash had settled. Here and there, near the river path, new blades pricked through and caught the light like pins. No one marked them aloud. The world had put them there and taken them away. A beat, not a lesson.

In the cave's shade, Risa slept against her caregiver's collarbone with a thumb in her mouth. Selura watched the small rise and fall of Risa's chest and felt the faint warmth answer once more, distant, like a light seen far off over water. It would come back. Not all at once. Enough.

Selura lifted a beam with Jarek and set it straight. She did not count who watched her. She did not need to. The day had put her where the people could see her, and they did.

Even in ruin the ground made room to begin. Between ash flakes, the first thin blades stood like small stitches. The land was already learning.

Chapter Seven

When the light outside the cave thinned to grey, the people gathered; no one called it a council. Cloaks were pulled close, knees drawn up, shoulders touching where the cave narrowed. Selura did not take a place of height. She lowered herself to the floor with a small, controlled breath, palms on her knees, her ribs giving that faint inward pull that came after a hard day's work. The warmth behind her eyes was banked now, not gone, just dimmed the way embers dim when the last wind has passed.

She did not begin with lessons. She asked what they had seen: the river, the hole, the ash, the way the ground had tried to keep Risa and then loosened its grip, the pale animal's prints in the burned meadow. Young ones spoke of the weight in their chests when the smoke closed in. Jarek, long in the arms and narrow in the face with sawdust still caught in the creases of his knuckles, told them how the beam had taken its place and how the grain had held. Their words went round in turns, until they thinned and frayed.

Selura rubbed once at the corner of her eye with the heel of her hand. She listened more than she spoke, and when she did speak, she kept her voice close to the ground, steady but quieter than she meant. The pull of Risa at the hole had left a small tremor in the base of her voice, barely there, but Bren noticed. Seyra's eyes flicked to her twice without comment. They would set cups; they would name who walked and who watched. No one would wander alone.

By the time the talking circle had thinned and the fire sank to coals, the cave held the softer sounds of people putting themselves back into place. Cord was being coiled, bowls stacked, someone laughed once and caught it back. This was the work after the work, the part no one would remember when they told it later.

Selura sat by the bowl where it always lived, the stone shelf cool beneath her hands. The beam she and Jarek had set earlier stood straight above, fresh-cut wood still smelling of sap. The day had put her where the people could see her; now it asked what she would do with that seeing.

She had spoken her share and heard theirs, and still the day would not let go. The river, the hole, Risa's thin voice from the dark, the sight of the pale ovals easing away across the far water; all of it sat behind her ribs like a hand that had not yet left.

When the last clatter and murmur faded, Selura set her fingers on the rim of the bowl. The water answered. The bowl darkened along the eastern rim; not by much, enough. The reflection of the cave roof and the dim smear of light that marked the mouth bent and thinned, as if the world had taken a breath and decided to show her something she had not asked to see. Two pale ovals eased into the darkened band, side by side.

"Earlier than it should be," Selura said. "And not alone." She let her fingers rest on the rim for a count. "We do not drag the whole cave out on a guess. Bren, take the lead on the east run; two should go with you. You watch, you count, you come back. No more than that."

Bren was already a shadow near the cave mouth, lips moving with the counts he would deny if anyone named them. He pulled a single coil of cord from its peg and set it on his shoulder; the heavier rolls of wedges and spare hooks he left where they were. Seyra gathered up a smaller sack, knots, a short mallet, two spare loops and pressed it into his hands with a troubled grin.

"Children to the cave," Eshra said, not loud, not soft. "Take them by the hands and walk. We are not running yet."

The bowl deepened again. Selura watched the dark along the eastern rim and let out a slow breath. "We stay with the east run," she said. "Spare line at the cave mouth, double coils. If the posts are loose, we wedge and pass the line gear forward."

Veyra came up with a coil over one shoulder and her hair tied ragged behind her head. The cord was the same thick river twist they carried on field runs, the kind that burned if it slipped. "I am fine on line," she said to no one and everyone. "Give me the long pull."

"Take staging first," Seyra answered, threading a belt with hooks and short lengths of spare cord. "You lay out what we need at the mouth, I will place the hands. We move quiet, not heavy. Bren is ahead; we keep to his pace."

"They are close," Veyra said. The words were flat, but her fingers tightened once on the coil. On another day her mouth might have found a smile. Not this one. She shifted the cord in her hands, feeling its weight, seeing in her head the stretch of open ground on the east run and the way the line might need to be thrown, looped or anchored if whatever walked in that band pressed the edge. This was not the calm work of setting a boundary. This was what the boundary was for.

Wind came once and went, one clean draft across the open ground where they were staging, enough to tug at loose coils and lift the edge of a cloak. Bren flinched and snapped on instinct. "Cut slack on the left, keep hands clear."

The coil in Veyra's hands jumped at the same moment, a length someone had pulled from the pegs too fast. A younger runner, knife already out to trim a trailing end, heard only the first word and turned sharply toward the nearest cord.

Veyra turned toward the call at the same moment the blade flashed. She did not move fast enough. The knife kissed her cheek from cheekbone to jaw, a thin bright line that opened all at once. She did not give the cave a sound. Her hand went to her face and came away red.

Seyra was there first with a strip of cloth and the tone she used for stubborn horses. "Hold still." She pressed the cloth in and up along the cut, her other hand firm on Veyra's shoulder.

Bren's count broke. "I said cut slack on the left," he started, his voice too loud for the close stone.

"You said cut," Veyra answered, voice low and clear around the cloth. "Say you saw where I was standing."

"I..." The runner who had done it had a face like a shuttered window. "I heard the call and thought you meant the loose end. I should have asked."

Eshra took in the cloth at Veyra's cheek, the red already seeping through, and the coil still cradled in her hands. "We still go," she said to the knot at the mouth. "Bren has the lead. Veyra, you are off the pull. You stay on staging."

"I am on line," Veyra said, the words tight.

"You cannot hold a long run like that," Seyra said, low but without softness. "Staging or you sit. Those are the options."

Veyra's shoulders went rigid. After a long count she gave the smallest nod she could manage.

Two runners took up the extra coil at the cave mouth. Eshra shoved a roll of wedges into Bren's chest and pressed the mallet into his free hand. "Keep it tight," she said. "You can return it when we're home."

"We are home," Bren said, too fast for the word to land. He bit it back as if it had been a boast and turned away before anyone could catch his eyes. At the cave mouth, the detachment settled into place behind him. "Two to a post, two to a coil," Bren said. "No drag."

They took the east run at a steady, practiced pace. Posts rose one by one, stone shoulders taking cord, knots set by hands that knew them.

Aravel ghosted ahead and then came back, always a little farther out than sense would advise. "There is something in the broken pasture," he told Bren, as if the report would bruise less in a steadier ear. "Past the break in the pasture. Not far."

"Show me how far," Bren said. "Do not make me guess from your face."

Aravel showed with his hands. "From the break to the first thistles; half a field."

They worked on. Bren stood where two cords crossed and tested their bend, watching the strand for small telltale signs that a knot is lying.

"We saw it," Jarek said, breath tight. "It is there! It is there!"

"What is 'it'?" Bren asked, hands on his work, feeding line across a post. "Give it a shape or I cannot believe you."

Jarek tried. "Twice the size of a man; hard to see. It looks like it takes the world into a kind of... age."

Bren left the post and stepped to the edge of the cord line. He sighted down the field.

Aravel pointed into the pasture. "There!"

"Is it leaning?" Bren said, as if the field were a lesson and not a threat.

"Not the body," Aravel said. "It is like the air around it reached first and forgot to tell the rest to follow."

They kept distance. No one crossed the cord line. The posts fixed a line of fact between their work and what lay beyond.

Bren pointed to a flat face of stone at his feet. "Show me the look."

Jarek squared the charcoal and sketched a band.

"That band swells when you move?" Bren asked. "Or does it pretend to listen and then do as it pleases?"

"It shifts," Jarek said. "It pulls a little toward motion, like it is curious. It held. And then it eased."

The field gave them a little more. A thistle on the left had sagged along its spines; the spurs looked less like knives and more like bad memory.

"Eyes on the line," Bren said, low. "If it comes to the cord, the grass will tell us first."

"You will know it by what you feel in your knees," he added, then winced at his own superstition, as if someone had heard him trust it.

Aravel's voice dropped to the pitch used around sleeping children. "Close enough to count. Not touching the line. Watching it."

At five paces the shape resolved. A bone frame inside a hanging hide, strips of ruined flesh slung from rib and shoulder, wet and stringing, the colour of old fat. Where it shifted, the tatters clung and peeled in slow threads. Two pits of black watched and did not blink.

Sound reached them late. A wet choking rose from inside the ruin, followed by a slow gurgle, as if something were taking in what it could not use. It drew a little toward them, a fraction at a time, the way warmth pulls a starving thing.

The grey spoil around it thickened. The cord under Bren's hand gave a small hum, almost kind, and the edge of the thing tightened as if the note hurt. It did not turn away. It gathered itself and pressed again.

When the spoil lapped the line, grass lost its green up the blade like stain up a wick. The top strand took on a dry pallor and rang once, high and thin, then held. The thing paused, drew back the length of a pace, and stood with its head slightly tipped, listening to what it could not bear or cross.

Jarek stepped back before he knew he had. Aravel set his heel to the turf and kept his hands clear of the cord. Bren did not move. "Stay to the line," he said, low. "Together."

It watched them a moment longer, where seconds seem to pass as years, and drifted away along the roll in the ground, its spoiled pale thinning behind it until the pasture remembered what it could.

"It watches everything," Bren said. "We do our work anyway."

He tapped the stone where Jarek had sketched and added a smaller shadow offset from the thicker side. "It leaned here when you moved?"

"Yes," Jarek said, the word small in the space between them.

"Lay a small bow into the memory cord," Bren said. "Keep the run true if it noses us." He raised his voice. "Hold the line! Aravel and Jarek, eyes up!"

They reset the wedges and slid the cord; the arc took and held, quiet and tight. Aravel and Jarek took one more look and came back with the same answer. "It is there. It knows we have a line."

"Good," Bren said, though nothing about it was. "Let it know we have a line, and let it wonder what waits behind it."

They finished that stretch and moved to the next, the world taking on that glassy moment before night completes itself. No one crossed the line.

The under-canopy kept a grey kind of light, as if the day had been filed thin and fitted between trunks. Iyren walked the edge paths where root-spines rose and stone ribs shouldered through the soil. Fallen metal leaves had settled into drifts of reddish dust; each step took him around them, not through, because rust carried a memory he did not trust to his own heels.

He did not turn back toward the face in the wood. Flame teaches. Ash frees. He decided it was enough.

He kept his eyes on his hands. In one palm he rolled a chip of resin until its scent rose, sharp as clean sap; in the other he weighed a thin flint and a loop of old cord he had cut from a dead line months ago. Only to remember he could.

Wind worked the mist in slow films between the columns of trees and slid away along a contour only it knew.

Iyren stopped where the wind had stalled and looked once into the gloom it left. He stepped off the path and took higher ground where the roots made reliable ladders.

The Silver Forest had its own arithmetic. He tried to set his columns against it: the cords and posts the village called safety, the bowl they called truth, the faces bent over that water with so much hope they mistook it for a face looking back.

The cords hold, he thought, but only hold. Hold long enough and people will call holding victory; they will build their lives against a line and forget the world beyond a line still shifts. Flame teaches. Ash frees.

He came to a shallow draw and crossed when the mist pulled aside. Not moving. Not many. Exactly where they belonged.

He gathered what he allowed himself: two resin lumps, a second flint, a handful of dry fibre from the interior of a dead vine that had once been rope. A brand stick he had prepared days ago, charcoal wrapped in thin cloth, went into his sleeve.

A ridge of rock gave him a seat. The urge that had walked with him since the far tree pressed close: strike the spark; set a small line against bark; teach the wood a lesson it would recognise. It would be so little, just a mark, a proof to himself that he had understood what was offered.

He did not strike. Not here. Not yet. He let the want rise and fall like a tide against stone and kept his palm open on his knee, the charcoal line dark in its channels.

The light shifted before any sound. Between two trunks something gathered itself out of the grey; high on the leg, fine in the frame, the head long in the muzzle like a river grazer. Its hide caught the dim light like fish-scale, a white-pearl sheen that turned the trunks faint in its reflection. Along the back a low ridge lifted and settled; no fur, a thin, clear comb that took the last colour of the day and laid it flat. The eyes were depthless, black to the core, ungiving.

When it stepped, the hooves pressed clean oval marks into the rust dust and lifted without sound.

Iyren stilled. He did not name it. He set his ribs to an even count and turned his palm so the mark faced the gap between the trunks. The head tipped once, a small answer, as if it understood he had seen it. A narrow breeze crossed and broke; the shape slipped, the pearled sheen went dull, and the seam closed as the trees remembered each other. He felt the after-look of it as a line drawn across him, faint and exact.

He turned his mind toward the line at home and saw it as the speaking tree had taught him to see it: not as a promise but as an argument scratched into earth. He pictured cords smoking clean, their learned memory burned free of the wrong lessons, the posts warmed so they would let go of rot and hold only the truth of what they were meant to anchor. Fire as grammar.

He imagined the conversations waiting if he carried this home too fast: Selura's careful eyes, Eshra's measured questions, Bren's stubborn pride. None of that mattered to the change the forest had put into his hands.

A distant shimmer rippled where the ground fell toward a creek he knew by smell more than map. Silver-leaf rust lay in a shallow fan at the base; he stepped around it.

He looked south and tried on the feeling of a teacher approaching a stubborn class: not to shame, not to wound, but to show a method that would end the lesson for good. He would show them a cord that had learned the right thing.

The day thinned to its last colour. His choice had already set. The cords are a lie of holding, he told himself, not aloud. There are truths you can only write with heat. He opened his hand one more time and saw the charcoal line dark in the channels of his palm. Fire would be his answer.

Iyren angled along a shelf of stone until the trees broke around a low square ruin. Rust from silver leaves pooled against the fallen corners, a dry red that stained the ridges of his boots.

Inside the wall the yard looked drained: soil ash-soft, colour fallen out of it, dead weeds sketching pale lines where the wind laid them. Something had eaten here until even the quiet wore thin.

He walked the long axis of the worst patch and counted his paces, then turned and counted across. A dead weed snapped under his boot and flaked into grey lines on the stone; a thin script the wind had taught it.

At the drain that once carried rain out of the yard, he found a stripe where colour had dropped another step toward ash. The grains had settled into a tight, speckled line that made the straight shape plain: the place where the eater's attention must have rested longest before it eased off and left a scar.

On the wall above, a lighter rectangle marked where a shield had hung. No object remained, only the negative. The absence was the lesson.

He turned toward a collapsed section and saw a ghost of a post in the ground: not wood, not stone, just a lighter cylinder of soil where something had refused to rot until it was convinced. He dug two fingers in and drew up a thread of old cord trapped in a crack. It turned powder-dry and fell through his hand like sifted flour.

He stepped back and looked at the yard as a diagram. It taught stillness and age to whatever stood near, until the lesson stayed.

He pictured a cord line running here. The memory of fibre would dry and tighten first; then knots would pretend to hold and, once taught otherwise, part without drama. Posts would loosen where the ground forgot how to clutch them.

Heat would teach better than rot, he thought. A line treated with flame remembers on purpose. Ash frees.

He crossed to a beam that had once roofed a walkway. He looked along its length and saw places where a patient hand could lay a narrow line of heat, no blaze, no spectacle, just enough to make the fibres keep their story against the eater's whisper. At the centre of the worst patch he found a coin-wide circle where even fungi refused to set.

He mapped in thought and footfall, shaping a passage that answered lightly to the place's taking. It would bring him through with more of himself intact.

A dry vine looped from one wall to another where someone had lashed a brace. Iyren touched the inner fibre and felt it part into powder, as with the cord. A small kit that could show a method when the time came.

The last of the evening found a way into the yard and laid a weak square on the far wall. He had seen what he needed.

He left by the route he had traced: slab to slab, foot on stone ribs, a long step over the stripe, then into the trees where silver leaves gave their rust back to the ground and the world remembered how to be ordinary. The lesson had to be shaped in his hands before he put it in anyone else's.

When he reached a clean rise between trunks, he sat with his back to greyed bark, the kit under his sleeve and the map of the yard still laid over his thoughts. He would show them how to end a lesson instead of pushing it off until it returned.

The dark gathered without drama. Iyren waited for his eyes to settle, then took the high ground toward another thinned place. What he knew was enough. Fire would make it plain.

The threshing stone lay where the field dipped and dusk pooled. It bore the grooves Dream had set on it, marks that read like work, and tonight it sat as if it had forgotten that purpose. The figure within the pale drifted near, its presence teaching the ground a faster age.

Selura set the detachment to a measured watch. No one crossed the cord line. No one stepped beyond a post. She set them at a slant so their bodies were not clean targets if the world decided to lean. She kept one palm near the line without touching it, feeling the charge of attention like weight behind the eyes.

At first the change came as small harms. The rim of the threshing stone eased along an arc, as if rubbed smooth by use it had not seen. Fine cracks webbed the face and turned to chalk that rose and fell in still air. At the foot, the soil slumped; roots that should have held gave way.

A runner came at a low sprint from the north posts. He kept to the farm path and spoke in clipped phrases. "North run is worrying. Top strand is drying. Knot looks true. The fibres are pale. We are setting wedges."

Eshra looked to Selura for the rest of the order. She nodded north. "Take Bren and five. Do not trade strength for speed. If the run asks more than you can give, fall to the second post and do not let it drag you forward."

Bren gathered the five and set off at a brisk pace. Seyra stayed at Selura's shoulder, eyes on the figure that had made the threshing stone forget its edges. "It is feeding," Seyra said.

A grey, mist-fine margin thickened toward the line. Grass blanched up each blade; shadows thinned. The line held and gave a small note. The figure edged closer until the sound caught in it: a hitch, a wet convulsion, then a slow turn of the head as if listening. It did not yield. It tested along the boundary for slack, kept its attention on the crew, and pressed more of its weight onto the threshing stone without looking away.

Another runner came from the north with dirt on her knees. "Anchor's seated, but the post is loosening. We wedged twice. The tension makes the top run sing." She grimaced and corrected herself. "It is tight."

Selura measured the stone with her eyes the way she would a face she loved and feared to lose. The round flattened along one side and then sagged, a dish beginning to learn it was a bowl. The centre powdered in a small grey bloom. She did not look away. If they survived this night, they needed this understanding as much as cord and posts.

To the north, the line began to answer to it. It stayed half seen, sliding along the boundary and pressing again, the way water works a seam. Eshra's team kept exact, hands-on knots, wedges set with short, true blows. Veyra came with a bundle under her arm, eyes already on the next gap.

Bren met her eye. "I need you at the cave. Dry gear, clean line. Come straight back."

She took the push as verdict. "Send someone else. I can work here."

"Carry it to the cave," he said again, not waiting for agreement. He turned to the post and checked the lash, jaw tight.

Veyra stood three posts down with the bundle on her hip and watched the fibres along the top run turn from the colour of wet flax to the colour of bone. She pressed her lips together and did not move for a count longer than reason.

At the anchor the top run began to fail. No snap, no cry; only a long, dry give. It thinned to a white seam and then opened. The fray showed two colours at once: the new chalk-pale it had learned and the old flax it had been. The second strand held. The third held. The memory in that stretch held a moment longer, then loosened at the edges.

The runner with dirt on her knees went pale to match the cord. "We are losing it." She ran, and this time did not keep to the farm path. She cut across the inner ground and reached Selura with her lungs working and her face set. "North is opening. I cannot be two people."

Selura kept her eyes on the threshing stone. Its working surface thinned to a chalk ring; the outer band held a moment, then followed and slumped. She fixed the sight where she would not lose it and gave the order she had known since the bowl first darkened.

"No repairs," Selura said. "Hold where you are. When Eshra calls, fall to the inner line. No one tries to be the line. We hold until I tell you to move."

"Heard," Eshra answered from the north. The word went down the crew like a tool passed hand to hand.

At the anchor the top run failed. No snap, no cry; only a long, dry give. It thinned to a white seam and opened. The second strand held. The third held. The north stretch of cord let go of its work and the pressure eased forward. Posts creaked in their sockets and then went quiet, not from strength but because nothing was left to take hold.

Selura's hands were steady and cold. The shape of the night changed in a way that was not about light. The threshing stone, all edges gone, sat like a grey moon fallen into dirt. What fed near it drew back a fraction, heavy and searching.

"Back to the cave," Selura said. It was not retreat. "We watch what comes next and make ready to close when the chance is given."

They withdrew without turning their backs, step by measured step. Veyra came last because no one had told her she could be first. Behind them the east field kept its new age; to the north, part of the village learned what a night without a cord line felt like.

Inside the cave the bowl had steadied to a picture no one wanted. Two strong ovals and a third troubling flicker opened and shut as if the night were closing a fist. Selura watched the surface gather that shape and keep it. She did not trust the bowl, only the asking. Tonight, the asking had been right twice.

Noise came ragged from the outer ground: feet on stone, people arriving along the known runs, faster than sense. Tools shook where they hung.

Selura turned from the bowl and took two memory knots from the top shelf. The hour was not for choosing.

"Sel..." Seyra began, but Selura was already moving, knots in hand, the path opening when people did not move fast enough.

The breach showed itself all at once. Not a hole, but a forgetting pushed through the north line until there was nothing to catch. Posts stood from habit, stripped of use. Grass inside the boundary had gone colourless and thread-thin; cords ended in white fringes, their learning torn off. A figure within its grey pale had crossed the dead edge and stood on village ground.

Jarek hung inside its reach.

His scream tore the cave and sent people stumbling. Hands came up without knowing what they meant to grab: post, cord, or friend. Someone sobbed his name. "Jarek!" Another voice broke. "Help him!" Eshra had him by the belt and could not win an inch; Bren locked onto Jarek's forearm and braced to a post that could lend nothing. The pale wrapped from Jarek's boots upward and the leather went to chalk under it. Wet choking worked inside the figure, a slow gurgle as if it were taking in what it could not use and refusing to stop.

"Hold," Jarek said once. Not loud. Meant for both of them. Then he screamed again, a raw, torn thing that made three people drop to their knees.

Selura did not step into the band. She felt Dream like a river behind a gate she could open only by agreeing to be part of what ran through. She paid it.

The Word rose in her. Dream answered as flood. Not light. Not heat. A surge of remembering larger than the cave, larger than her. She gripped the knots and set a direction, and that force ran through bone and ground. Stone underfoot thrummed. Posts answered. The cord ends lifted as if a hand drew them up from below.

Her knees went loose at the first touch. She pictured the cord the day it was first strung: fibres clean, posts true, people believing. Dream ran toward that memory and poured through her like the river when the thaw lets go.

"Now," she said, voice not her own for a heartbeat. Seyra caught it and fed the long draw into the heads at the posts. Between hands and knots a line took shape; for a count it did not exist and then it did, a single taut memory laid back across the opening. The air went hard, then rang. Dust lifted in a circle around Selura and blew outward. The bowl on its shelf sang like struck stone.

A thin brightness answered from the cave mouth. Dream-lilies along the seep woke as if pulled up by a tide, their cups opening all at once, lantern-pale. A low note threaded out of them and found the cord, a simple line that carried and held. Petals took on the look of lit bone. Where the Word pressed, their singing rose a step and the grey along the ground shivered, as if sound itself were teaching it to thin. The lilies kept time for her hands.

More figures came. One rose at the edge of the breach. Another slid from the threshing stone's direction. Their pales swelled to meet the new run and pressed until the heads at the posts took strain.

The one on Jarek did not let go.

The pale climbed him in a slow tide. Cloth thinned beneath Bren's grip. Fibres went to dust along Jarek's sleeve. Skin dulled where the grey tightened, as if ash were blooming under it. The choking inside the figure grew thick, a swallow that never finished. Jarek's weight changed in Eshra's hands, heavy, then oddly light, as if the world were deciding how much of him to keep. Patches of him stilled mid-motion, a wrist, a cheek, a strip along the ribs, edges too exact for the living.

"Jarek," Eshra said, the voice people use at bedsides and graves.

The line held, but not for him. The pale drew once more. Jarek's belt loosened into powder. Bren's fingers shut on nothing. Eshra pulled and the pull had nothing to answer. Jarek went out of the world with the sound of stones easing. For a small count the space kept his shape. Then it was only ground. In the centre lay the neat grey of a print and a single wedge, fallen from his hand, a tool that had not learned how to be older fast enough to follow him.

Someone wailed. A runner tried to rush the gap and was caught by two others, babbling, shoulders shaking. "He was right there. He was right—" The words would not finish.

Selura lifted the knots and did not lower them. The river in her rose higher. The Word pressed through her throat and chest until the air around her shivered. The cord hummed in answer along the full sweep; wedges seated with a sound like teeth setting. A wind came from nowhere, one hard circle that burst outward from where she stood and drove the grey back along the ground. Grass stood up as if remembering how. The pale on the approaching figures wrinkled, tightened, then went thin.

She drove Dream along the imagined path of the cord until the thought had weight enough to be fact. Posts answered. Hands answered. The rebuilt top run tightened to a clean lay; knots seated; blows short and true. For a count the pale refused to understand. Then it did. The second figure slid backward and tried to gather itself. The third faltered, found no purchase, and let the edge of the run push it like a slow tide going out.

"Tie it," Selura said, or someone said it for her after her first voice ran out. Repairs moved under the cover she made. People worked while weeping. Bren's mouth formed words he did not say. Eshra set a knot and had to set it again because his hands shook.

Veyra stood a post's length off the line with the cloth stripe dark on her cheek and the bundle still in the crook of her arm. The lilies' low note found her bones. She looked past the work and past the field, to where the edge paths broke toward the Silver Forest. Iyren's name did not leave her mouth. She set the bundle down on a flat stone and did not pick it up again.

The remaining figures edged back beyond the outer field, their pales shrinking to the size they wore when they did not find motion. They did not vanish. They kept to the distance the cord allowed and waited to see if the village would forget. That was their talent.

When the line was a line again, Selura opened her hands. The knots fell into her lap. Silence followed, heavy as pressure. No one quite looked at her. Not yet. Not the same way.

People turned toward Jarek's absence and then away, the way eyes avoid holes. No one picked up the wedge. Seyra pressed a cloth into Selura's hand and it came away red in a telling smallness. Eshra stood and did not quite sway. Bren counted and found them all still there except the one who was not.

"We are closed," someone said at last, and the words moved through the cave like a verdict more than a cheer.

Selura tried to stand and found the floor preferred her. "Cave," she managed. "Tools away. We count, then we stop." She touched the knots as if to be sure they were still there and not a story she had borrowed and returned.

Veyra stood a little apart, the cloth stripe on her cheek gone dark, eyes refusing anyone's help. The space between her and the crews felt like new rope strung between posts, useful and ready to cut a hand that grabbed it.

They walked in a broken order toward the cave with the cord at their backs, a taut curve in the dark on shoulders of stone. That was not its work. The lilies dimmed by slow degrees and folded. One set of footfalls did not return with the rest. Veyra had already taken the inner path toward the trees.

At the first post Selura looked once over her shoulder at the north run.

The night did not end. That would have to be enough until morning decided what it wanted.

Chapter Eight

The figure's stink still fouled the valley, a sour rot that clung to the back of the throat. Under it, faint and stubborn, the earth carried a clean, damp note. People kept their voices low outside the cave. Wrong words felt dangerous.

They carried Selura just before first light. Mira walked backward, Selura's head in her arms, jaw locked tight. Bren bore most of the weight, shoulders rounded, boots careful on slick stone. The cords strung along the cave's walls gave off a low hum that rose and fell with Selura's weak pulse.

Her body showed the cost. Veins stood out dark along her throat and wrists, gathering at the burned circles in her palms. The whites of her eyes were raw around pupils blown wide. Fine cracks ran from her temples down the sides of her neck, as though light had once forced its way out there and left the skin split.

Mira laid her near the Homefire. Heat rolled from Selura's skin. Before Mira's fingers reached her brow they were already prickling. When she brushed ash from Selura's hair, the texture beneath felt too thin, as if the body had been woven one time too many.

"Her veins are turning against her," Bren said quietly. "They do not look like they belong to a living body."

"They belong to what she faced," Mira answered. Her voice rasped. "And it did not finish its work."

Eshra settled at Selura's side, staff across her knees. She closed her eyes and held her hand a finger's width above Selura's brow. Heat throbbed there in slow, heavy beats that did not match the shallow rise of her chest. The cords had hummed in that same uneven rhythm.

"Dream is not finished with her," Eshra said. "If it had taken her, there would be nothing. This is not nothing."

Seyra knelt near Selura, inspecting her hands. She did not touch the burned rings. Instead, she traced the air above one with the tip of her nail. The grey skin around the circle had lost its angry shine. Deep under it, something darker pulsed once, then lay still.

"The knots pulled more than they were meant to hold," Seyra murmured. "They took her full weight and did not break. Dream rode those cords and did not let go."

No one replied. Those who had crowded the doorway drifted out one by one, leaving only the ones who knew how to sit through a long, uncertain wait.

Day crawled. Mira wiped Selura's face with river water and counted each rise of her chest. Bren kept the fire low and steady, feeding it with small pieces of wood. From time to time he set his hand flat on the ground beside Selura's shoulder, anchoring himself more than her.

"You said that when the forest turned," Bren answered. "You said it when she walked through echo-sick air. She is still here."

"Here is not the same as whole," Eshra said.

As the light outside thinned, the hum in the stone deepened. Its even note sank into a slow, heavy throb that seemed to rise from beneath the cave rather than from the cords alone. The air felt stretched. The Homefire's flame pulled inward, thin and bright.

Mira looked up. "Do you feel that?"

Bren spread his fingers against the floor. The vibration ran up his arm. "The cords are listening," he said. "Or she is."

Selura's chest rose and fell in a heavy rhythm. Sweat beaded at her temples and traced thin paths into the cracks along her neck. Her fingers twitched once. The blackened rings in her palms darkened further, as if soot had been driven down into them.

"The deep sleep," Eshra said quietly. "Dream takes her now."

No one tried to stop it. There was nothing left to do but watch. The sound in the stone thinned to a single low tone and slipped past hearing.

For Selura, it became ground.

The fevered dark pressed over her, reshaping itself until she found herself not at home surrounded by kin but in a whole new world that seemed to mirror her own.

She stood beside the river as she always had, yet the water ran uphill. The current crawled back toward its source, dragging stones and broken branches against the slope. Above, the stars broke apart and drifted like scattered embers, painting constellations she did not know; they hung too low and too bright. When the reversed river pulled at their reflections, pieces of those patterns cracked off and fell as glass into the water.

She walked along the bank through a world turned inside out. Stones lay on their underside. Roots curled in air like exposed ribs. In the shallows, fish twisted through the current in broken angles, their movements just out of time with the water, as if Dream had not finished making them.

Far off, mountains folded in on themselves, their ridges curling inward as if something beneath them kept trying to rise and remake them in a different shape, never quite settling.

Far downstream, people clung to a shore that crumbled under them. Without thinking, Selura reached out. Light flared from her burned palms, stretching into a narrow path across the water. Those closest seized it and stumbled to safety. Those behind stepped where there was no ground and one by one, they fell.

The river swallowed them whole, yet their shapes rose from the surface in thin, bright threads and darted themselves into the cracked sky. The shore that remained held. Fields there were green and still. Children laughed along an edge that had no bodies.

Suddenly, the vision tore.

The river stilled. Its surface hardened into a perfect, dark mirror that showed nothing back. No leaf floated on it. No wind touched it. The air smelled of rain that never quite arrived, a promise held but never spent. The banks held no prints. Every mark that should have proved someone had stood there blurred and slipped away. The quiet did not heal. It leeched. The longer she looked, the more it felt as if the world were being smoothed flat so nothing sharp could catch on it again.

Selura listened for the river's old song and heard only her own pulse, slowed and muffled. The silence smoothed everything it touched. Fear eased. Hunger dulled. Joy, too. Edges blurred until nothing sharp remained.

Again the dream shifted, not into anything new but deeper into the same unraveling. She stood in the current. The backward flow dragged at her legs, heavy and cold. Her shadow did not fall behind. It slid forward, stretched over the surface and sank at the centre of the stream. There it thickened into a single dark line that held light to one side and deepened dark on the other.

The pull of it ran up through her bones. Her skin burned along her purple veins. Her chest felt braced open, ribs turned into a frame for something that was no longer only hers.

Then the sky split from horizon to height. In the tear, Selura glimpsed a seam: not an empty space but a presence that refused every shape. A black seep poured from that space, thickening the river with every beat.

From the seam began the sound of a rasp, which swelled into a wet, choking gargle. The noise crawled into the bones of the mirrored world, rattling stone, shaking light loose from the air. The narrow path of mercy trembled. The still mirror buckled. The sky darkened. Her own shadow-line frayed where it held light and darkness apart.

A whisper pushed through the seam and into her mind, vibrant and deeply wrong. It gathered itself around her thoughts until it broke into a single, clear meaning she could not refuse. Nymire. The knowing of it sat in her like a weight, the sense of something that waited whenever cost went unpaid and wounds were left to deepen out of sight.

Her knees hit the riverbed. Shards of fallen sky bit into her skin. She tried to speak the word she had used on the waking riverbank, the one that had closed the line. Her mouth formed the first clean sound. The second filled with the taste of rot. The third scattered as she cried out.

The dream cracked again.

Her scream broke loose. In the distance, Dream Lilies screamed. The piercing note rippled through her consciousness, a sharp thread drawn tight enough to snap. Selura woke.

The cave where Selura lay did not stay still. A single violent tremor ran through the stone, lifting dust from the ceiling and scattering ash across the firepit. Men and women at the entrance grabbed for the walls as the floor heaved under them, as if the world itself had flinched.

The stone quieted slowly after the tremor, settling back into itself in small, uneven steps. Dawn thinned the dark at the entrance, its light sliding over the dust still drifting from the ceiling and the ash shaken loose around the firepit. The coals barely held their glow.

Mira, Bren, Seyra, and Eshra were the only ones who remained in Selura's chamber. Across the cave, the rest of the village had resumed their morning in their own spaces, unsettled by the tremor but keeping to their work. Even so, more than a few paused to listen for anything that might follow.

Selura drew in air so sharply that Bren jerked awake. The bowl of river water beside her bed trembled. A single ripple ran across its surface and died at the rim.

"Mira," Bren said.

Mira was already on her knees, leaning over Selura. "Selura. Hear me."

Selura's eyes opened.

For a moment she stared past them at the roof, trying to remember which world this was. Smoke-stained stone, familiar knots along the walls; at last, her gaze found Mira's face.

"You are back," Mira said. It came out as statement and plea both.

Selura tried to speak. Her throat rasped. The second attempt held. "How long?"

"Since you fell?" Eshra asked. "One night. Enough for Dream to decide whether to keep you."

Selura exhaled, thin and tight. "It did not ask."

"No," Eshra said. "It rarely does."

Bren slid an arm behind Selura's shoulders and eased her upright. The motion exposed her hands. In the pale light the burned circles were stark, black centres ringed with hard, uneven flesh. Faint glimmer lay deep in them like embers buried under stone.

Selura stared. For a heartbeat her own body felt like something she had borrowed.

The bowl at her side rippled once, the water bending toward her instead of away.

"You remember," Eshra said. "At least some of it."

"Yes." Her voice steadied. "Enough."

A dark line pulsed under her skin, a reminder that some part of the seam had not left her.

"Tell us what matters," Eshra said. "Not every step. Just the shape."

Selura closed her eyes briefly, sorting horror from use.

"The river ran wrong," she said. "It pushed upstream. The sky hung too low. Stones that should have held gave way. The ground opened where it should have stayed whole."

"People were sliding into the current from the bank," she said. "I reached out, light went out to them before my hands could catch; they went under. When they rose again, they were only light and did not fall back."

Bren swallowed. "And the shore?"

"It held," Selura said. "Greener. Quieter. With fewer people on it."

"Mercy that chooses who remains," Eshra said.

Selura nodded once. "Then the river went flat," she said. "It turned to a mirror. No song. No pull. Nothing in it reached for anything. It did not feel healed. It felt emptied."

Eshra waited a moment. "What happened then?"

"The mirror cracked," Selura said. "It broke all at once, and the water came back. Cold. Pulling backward."

Selura's fingers tightened on the pelt at her back.

"I stood in the current," she said. "The pull came from both sides. One bank wanted to drown the other. I held between them. If either side moved, it would have flooded the rest. The river treated me like a line pinned in the middle."

She glanced down at her hands.

"It did not fix anything," she said. "It only kept both sides from swallowing one another. Long enough for something else to arrive."

Bren frowned. "What else?"

The sky opened," Selura said. "A seam, bright at the edges. Something pushed through it. Black seep came with it and ran into the river. The water thickened where it touched."

Mira's fingers tightened on hers. "You said you did not see it."

"I did not," Selura said. "Only the wrongness. And the sound it made."

"What sound?" Eshra asked.

"The rasp," Selura said. "That choking, broken sound. The world bent when it came. Light shook loose. The river moved as if everything were being pushed out of its right shape."

Mira steadied her. "You tried to stop it."

"I tried to speak the old word from the riverbank," Selura said. "It would not come. My mouth filled with rot. The sound died before I could shape it."

"What happened then?" Seyra asked.

"The dream cracked," Selura whispered. "Everything inside me pulled tight when it broke. No new hurt, only the strain I already carried."

A faint tremor ran through her hands. The blackened rings caught the thin morning light.

"It stayed with me when the dream fell away," she said. "Not a voice. Not a shadow. Only the knowing of it."

The cords along the wall creaked softly, as if the air inside the room shifted with her words.

Eshra did not look away. "Then give it a name," she said. "Do not leave it as a weight and a smell. Name it so we can point at it when it comes."

The word had been waiting at the back of Selura's mind since Iyren had stepped out of the forest, reeking and half himself. It sat coiled behind every crooked dream she had not understood.

She tasted it once, then let it out.

"Nymire," she said.

The name hit the air hard.

The coals in the firepit dimmed, then flared. The knots along the walls shivered in a single, clear tremor. In the bowl beside Selura's bed, the water rippled backward from rim to centre, then went still.

"You are certain," Eshra said.

"Yes," Selura replied. "It is not Dream turned sour. It feeds. It takes from what Dream sends through the seams. It wants the world stilled so it can take all of it."

"You think it will come again," Bren said.

"It will," Selura answered. "It pressed through the seam in the dream. If nothing stands in its way, it will find the places where the world thins."

"So you mean to stand where the word failed," Eshra said.

Selura drew a slow breath. "I tried it because I had nothing else," she said. "The first word. The one that answered the river and made this cave. I thought it might hold. But in the dream it broke in my mouth. I could not shape it. The rot drowned it."

Mira's jaw tightened. "You are not a tool," she said. "You are ours."

"I know," Selura said softly. "But the burden does not care what place I hold among us."

Eshra studied her. Dawn caught her face fully now. The child who had played at the river's edge still lived behind her eyes, but something steadier sat with her.

"The Nymire has a name now," Eshra said. "And the seams have someone watching them. None of this asked what we wanted. All we can choose is how we stand with you."

She reached for Selura's wrists and lifted her hands, palms up. The burned circles stared back, stark and unhealed.

"There is sorrow in this," Eshra said. "But there is work waiting. We will share it."

Selura let out a long breath, and her shoulders eased.

"Then help me hold," she said.

None of them promised they could stop what was coming. They answered in the ways they had: Bren's hand tightening on her shoulder, Mira's thumb brushing once across her knuckles, Seyra's quiet nod, Eshra's grip firm on her wrists.

Outside, light crept down the cave mouth and across the riverbank, catching on ash and new green. A thin bright line drew itself toward whatever waited beyond the seams.

Outside, the cords stirred again, as if waiting for someone else to move next.

Dawn found Veyra at the far edge of the meadow, where the last thin grasses sloped toward the Silver Forests. Her feet ached from the night's walk, but the ache felt cleaner than the tight looks and clipped words she had left behind. A few seldom dream-lilies, stragglers drifted too far from home, glimmered weakly in the damp earth. Their light looked out of place here, thin and uncertain, as if even they were reluctant to approach the trees.

She touched the cloth across her cheek. She had tried to sleep after he left. Her body refused it.

Behind her, the meadow still lay in half-dark. She imagined the crews waking, voices gathering around Selura when Dream finally released her. They would find Veyra missing and fold the absence into work. Bren would mutter once, tired and sharp, and then move on. He had already pushed her from the cord without seeing her. Necessary, he had said. Staging. Bring clean gear. As if distance could keep her from what she already knew.

Iyren had walked away carrying something Dream itself could not hold. If he kept walking, only the forest would answer him.

He will not come back on his own, she thought. Not now.

Veyra shifted the small pack higher on her shoulder and crossed the last stretch of meadow toward the tree line.

A shallow puddle pooled between two roots, and the water caught her reflection for an instant. First she looked older, weathered in years; then younger, like only a sprite; then only herself again. The surface of still water liking tricks of its own.

She stepped past the shallow pool and paused at the final post. The cord was cold under her fingers, the fibers drawn tight from the night wind. No hum, no memory, just the faint tension of work left behind. She let the line fall.

"If you will not come back," she murmured, "I'll find you."

She stepped fully beneath the trees; the forest waited.

Mist slid low between roots, rising just above her boots. The quiet held itself too carefully, as if the whole place braced against the next breath. Veyra felt the weight of it settle along her ribs. She did not look back. Her place, for this stretch of time, lay ahead.

The trunks stood close and pale. In a small depression beneath one tree, a scatter of grey powder clung to the ground. Veyra crouched and brushed two fingers through it. Heat lived there, faint but wrong for morning.

"You were here," she whispered.

The forest thickened. The mist climbed to her knees. No birds called. No insects stirred. The absence pressed against her ears until her own heartbeat sounded too loud.

She reached a narrow stream where the water barely moved. Along its edge, reeds that should have been green stood brittle and colorless, clear as thin glass. When she touched one, it chimed—a sharp, fragile note—and fell to dust.

In the mud beside it lay a footprint.

Pressed deep. Broad toes. A notched heel she knew as well as her own. The edges had hardened to black, as though heat had licked outward after he stepped away. Veyra leaned close. Warmth still gathered in the print's center.

"Please come back," she breathed.

Mist tightened around her, folding sound inward. Something answered.

Not a voice. Not a word. A thin, frayed sound drifted between the trees like laughter stripped of its warmth. It brushed both ears without choosing a direction.

"I hear you," she said quietly. "And I'm coming."

She crossed the stream. Water bit through her boots. Behind her, the last of the glass-reed stalks chimed once more and collapsed.

The trees pressed closer. Roots knotted underfoot. Heat pulsed beneath her palm when she steadied herself against a trunk, as though something within the wood exhaled slow and unwilling. The air tasted of resin layered with a sour edge, like rot waiting its moment to begin. Under it lay a scent she knew too well: scorched sap, sharp and stubborn; Iyren's scent after any fire.

She pressed her fingers to her cheek until the burn eased and moved on.

A faint trail thickened as she climbed a small rise. Ash clung to the bases of several trees, gathering in loose shapes nearly like footprints. Iyren's stride was coming apart in the earth, each step less certain than the last, as though he no longer knew how to be held by the world.

Another print waited beneath an arch of two leaning trunks; deep, cracked outward from the center. Veyra touched the ground. Warmth met her.

"Iyren... you're ahead of me."

Something shifted deeper in the forest.

Not a step. A weight. A slow adjustment, like a creature turning its attention. Mist stirred around her boots.

Veyra stood still. Fear crept up her ribs. She swallowed it. Iyren had walked this way burning without flame. She would not turn aside.

She moved toward a narrowing where branches crossed overhead, forming a throat of wood and drifting mist. Warm air flowed through it, carrying resin, smoke, and that sharpened sour note. Beneath it all lay the faint trace of Iyren himself.

"If you're still yourself," she whispered, "I'm coming."

The trees closed behind her.

The world narrowed to mist, heat, and the fading memory of Iyren's steps. Veyra walked on, steady as a vow, drawn toward whatever waited in the heart of the Silver Forests.

She set her hand on a rough trunk to steady herself.

The path ahead grew uneven, his steps dragging deeper into the soil as if his weight had changed. "You're still ahead of me," she murmured. "But not by much."

The air in front of her wavered. Between two close-set trunks, mist thinned to reveal a crack that did not belong to bark or stone or sky. It hung in the air at shoulder height; a narrow seam of silver brightness edged in dark. Veyra stopped short.

She had never heard any of the elders speak of seams. She had no old story to hang this on. It stood in front of her as if someone had dragged a knife through the air and the cut had never healed. Her chest tightened. The smart thing would have been to turn back. Go home. Tell someone who knew what to do with a crack in the world. Instead, she edged around it.

The seam cracked open a few inches as she passed. Strange light began to emanate from its fissure. It did not pull at her. It hung, patient and wrong. As if the world itself was showing signs of wear.

Suddenly, laughter drifted between the trunks. At first she thought it might be Iyren's, the breathy almost-chuckle he gave when a fire caught better than he expected. This sound stretched too thin. It scraped along the bark and came back to her in pieces, as if someone far away snatched the shape of laughter and forgot to leave anything warm inside it.

She looked back at the seam, convincing herself it must be this anomaly producing such audible guise. But even with the reasoning socked away she could not help but keep her head on a swivel.

Amid the scared trees, Iyren's trail sharpened. She found another footprint pressed into half-hardened ground. Ash had crept up the sides of the impression and fused there, leaving a raised edge. A few steps beyond that, near a root ledge, a shard of fired clay lay near a root, its curve and colour unmistakable. Veyra stooped and picked it up.

It was the size of a small river stone, worn from long handling. One side still smelled faintly of smoked broth and herbs. Iyren had carved that gourd-bowl a year ago, complaining the whole time that he was better with flame than knife. She had teased him until he smiled and finished the last cut clean.

Now the gourd was broken. The fracture was not neat. Heat had split it from within, leaving the edges bubbled and black.

"What did you walk into?" she whispered.

She set the shard back where she had found it and kept moving.

The forest ahead felt wrong. The trunks leaned inward, their bark pale and cracked where the light had been drained away. Roots bled resin that had turned dark and sluggish, and the ground itself seemed to breathe in slow, uneven pulls. She passed through a stretch where Dream's touch had been stripped bare, leaves hung colourless, the air sour with the scent of things half-alive. It was a wound that had tried and failed to close.

Beyond it, the forest grew darker. Roots pushed through soil that no longer knew which way to grow, and the air carried the taste of metal and damp stone. She could feel where the world had sagged under his passing, as though Dream itself had drawn back from that place.

Then, between two leaning trunks, she saw him. He stood with his back half-turned, one hand braced on a tree, the other hanging loose at his side. His shoulders slumped as if he had walked for days without rest. Fine red rust dusted his cloak and caught in his hair. Even from a distance she could see how the line of his body had changed, tense where it had once been easy, held too carefully, like someone trying not to shake.

"Iyren," she called.

The name left her before she had time to think. For a heartbeat nothing moved. Then he flinched. He turned slower than she expected, as though the air had thickened around him. His face looked wrong in small ways: his eyes a little deeper, lines of strain across his brow that had not been there before. His gaze slid past her once, unfocused, as if she were another trick of light caught in the mist.

"You're not real," he said hoarsely. "You're another one of its shapes."

Veyra froze. "It?"

He blinked hard, once. Twice. His eyes found her fully on the third try. For an instant something old and familiar surfaced, surprise, relief, the quiet brightness that had always come when he spotted a friend near the fire.

"Veyra," he said. The sound of her name this time carried weight. "You should not be here."

"And you should?" she shot back, heat flaring under her exhaustion. "You walked into the Silver Forest alone. What did you expect me to do, sit by the knots and hope you wandered home?"

He laughed once, a rough, broken thing. His shoulders tightened. "You were supposed to stay where Dream can still see you."

"Dream hasn't looked my way in a long time," she said. "You know that." She took a step closer. The air around him felt warmer than it should, not with fever but with a low, banked heat that seemed to gather under his skin. "What happened to you?"

"I saw more than I was meant to," he answered. For a breath his voice was calm, almost clear. "There are things in these trees that do not belong to your river. I followed them."

The words might have been a warning. They might have been a confession. They sat between them like both.

"Then come home," Veyra said. "Whatever you think you've found, it can not be worth dying for."

A flicker crossed his face. For a heartbeat he looked unsettled, almost tempted. Then something behind his eyes hardened.

"Home is already burning," he said. "You just haven't seen the spark yet."

The certainty in his tone chilled her more than the words. He lifted a hand as if to reach toward her, then let it fall uselessly to his side.

"Go back," he murmured. "If you stay with me, you'll be caught in it."

"I'm already caught," she said. "You left, and I'm still there." She swallowed. "I'm not turning around."

The forest answered before he could. A wet gasp rolled through the trees, too low to be wind or beast. The sound crawled along bark, shook rust from the branches above them, and dug claws of cold along Veyra's spine.

Iyren's head snapped toward the sound. "Run!" he said, and this time there was no fracture in his voice. Only command.

Their bodies moved before their thoughts caught up. Veyra spun and bolted in the direction they had come, feet slipping on slick roots. Iyren's steps thudded close behind. The gasp came again, louder, laced with a wet gargle she knew too well from the night prior.

She risked a glance over her shoulder. Between the trunks, something massive moved, a lumpen shape that bent the mist around it. No clear edges, only glistening folds and the sucking pull of its passage. Wherever it went, silver bark blackened and peeled away.

"Keep going," Iyren shouted. "Do not look back!"

They crashed through a stand of saplings that had already begun to bow away from some unseen centre. One snapped under Veyra's weight. Another caught her shoulder and spun her sideways. She stumbled; Iyren's hand closed around her forearm and hauled her upright before she hit the ground.

The air thickened, heavy with rot and the bitter tang of severed resin. At last, the ground pitched downward and the trees thinned. They burst into a narrow gully choked with mist. The sound of the creature's passage faltered at the edge of the drop, as if whatever mass it carried did not care to test the slope.

Veyra and Iyren tumbled the last few spans, sliding on loose stones and ash. They landed hard at the bottom; air knocked from their lungs. For several heartbeats there was only their breathing and the distant, frustrated rasp of the figure that hunted them. The sound retreated by slow degrees, swallowed again by the vastness of the wood.

Veyra rolled onto her back and stared up at the thin strip of yellowed sky visible between the leaning trunks. Her chest burned. Her legs shook.

"Still think I should have stayed by the river?" she managed.

Iyren let out a breath that might almost have been a laugh. He lay beside her; face turned toward the gully's wall. "You pick a bad time to be right," he said. The roughness had not left his voice, but for a moment something easier slipped through it.

They lay there until their breathing slowed. When Veyra pushed herself upright, her arms trembled. Iyren rose more slowly, one hand pressed flat against the ground as if feeling for some pulse under the stone. Whatever he found seemed to steady him.

He looked not back toward the way they had come, but deeper into the trees beyond the gully. The trunks there leaned in strange angles. Mist pooled heavier along the ground. The air that drifted up from that direction carried the faint smell of iron and old smoke.

"There's more ahead," he said quietly. It was not wonder in his tone. Not exactly dread, either. Something like recognition. "It is waiting."

"Then we go together," she said.

She did not say 'because I'm afraid to let you out of my sight.' She did not say 'because if you walk into whatever made that crack in the sky, it will take you alone.' Instead, she stood, dusted ash from her hands, and adjusted her pack strap like they were setting out on an ordinary scouting run.

Iyren glanced at her, something unreadable in his expression. "You should still turn back," he said. "This could be your last chance."

"No," she answered. "I made my choice when I left the meadow."

Whatever waited there had already taken hold of Iyren. Veyra could feel it in the way his shoulders squared, in the way his steps never wavered. She moved with him anyway, following his path into the forest, knowing whatever waited there had already taken hold of him.

For a moment she could have swore she saw a glimpse of the boy he had been. Apart of her wanted to believe he was still in there. Iyren's head lifted sharply; his gaze turned away from her, snapping toward the trees ahead as if some subtle current had shifted in the air. Veyra felt nothing, no wind, no change in the mist but he straightened as though someone had called his name from a distance.

"It is this way," he murmured.

Her mouth went dry. "Iyren, slow down. We do not know what's..."

"I do." He interrupted.

His tone wasn't hard; in fact, it seemed distant. Like the words traveled a long way to reach his tongue. "It is waiting." Said Iyren.

Veyra's arms lifted, she pushed herself to her feet anyway. "Then you're not going to meet it alone."

He did not argue. That, more than anything, unsettled her. They climbed out of the gully into a corridor of trees where the air felt thicker, heavy with warmth and silence. Iyren walked with unnerving surety. His boots found the firmest ground without searching. His shoulders squared as though some internal tension had finally found a direction to flow. Veyra kept close at his side, eyes flicking from root to root, from trunk to trunk, searching for any sign that the Nymire had followed them or that something worse waited ahead.

The light changed as they walked. It did not brighten or dim so much as thin, it filtered through the canopy in narrow ribbons that picked out small patches on the forest floor. Everything beyond those bands looked faintly blurred, as if distance itself were refusing to resolve. Veyra's head buzzed with the wrongness of it but she did not let herself slow.

She watched Iyren's profile as they moved. His jaw clenched and unclenched. His lips moved once without sound, like he stood answering a question she had not heard. Each time her hand brushed his arm in the close quarters between trees, warmth pulsed beneath his sleeve: low, banked, like an old hearth still holding coals under its dust.

"Tell me what you're hearing," she said quietly. He startled, as though remembering she was there. "It is not... words, exactly." His brow furrowed. "More like... a pull. A promise. I can almost understand."

"Promises from things that live in this forest sound like a bad trade," Veyra muttered. He almost smiled at that. Almost.

"You haven't heard this one." He said.

"Good." Her voice came sharper than she intended. "I do not want to."

The trees ended without warning. Their roots gripped the rim of a vast chasm that dropped into nothing. The air felt heavier here, the space ahead too large to name. Veyra stopped at the edge.

A platform jutted out before her, broad enough for several people to stand side by side. Its surface was smooth and blacker than night, swallowing even the pale light that reached it. The texture was not stone, not metal— something older, something that refused reflection. Jet.

She crouched and touched it. The surface drank the faint colour from her skin. No warmth, no chill. Only absence.

Beyond the platform stretched emptiness. She could not tell if it was distance or fog that hid the other side. Then, through that grey expanse, a dim light trembled.

"Iyren," she whispered.

He joined her at the edge. Together they watched the flicker grow until it became several points of orange, distant and unsteady. When the wind shifted, the light flared, and she saw the shape of tall pillars rising from the unseen ground. Metal bowls crowned their tops, each holding a fire that burned but gave little heat.

"They're flames," she said.

"I see them," Iyren murmured. His eyes narrowed, reflecting the faint glow. "They're calling."

He stepped closer to the edge; his gaze fixed on the farthest flame. The air around him seemed to tighten. For a long moment he said nothing, as if listening for something only he could hear.

Then he spoke. The word was low, shaped more by intent than sound.

A spark answered across the gulf. The fires brightened, threads of light stretching from one bowl to the next until they joined in a single line. From that line, a span of ember and living flame unfolded, crossing the void and anchoring itself to the jet beneath their feet.

The bridge pulsed faintly, alive but calm, its surface giving off a soft, steady glow. Veyra reached out and brushed it with her fingers. The warmth surprised her, it was gentle, almost human. Iyren stepped onto it first.

"It will hold," he said without turning.

Veyra hesitated, the gulf yawning beneath her, the ruin's far side hidden by fog. Then she followed.

The ember light carried them forward, and as they walked, the fog ahead began to thin. What emerged was not landscape but structure; vast walls of jet, blacker than the platform, rising into shadow. Two of the great pillars loomed near the gate, their fire bowls burning steady above. The ruin waited, silent and immense, its surface drinking the light that sought to touch it.

Two colossal doors dominated the ruin's front wall, rising at least three times their height. They met in a single, razor-straight seam down the center of the walkway. The doors had no handles, no visible hinges. The stone around them bore no mark of weather. This place did not feel ancient so much as indifferent to time altogether.

Iyren walked toward the doors. Veyra reached for his arm. "Wait."

He paused, not because of the word, she thought but because some part of him still knew how to respond when someone asked him to. "What if whatever's waiting in there isn't something you can walk away from?" she asked.

His throat worked once. Twice. "I think that's the point."

Before she could answer, he pressed his palm along the seam. The doors exploded inward; wind roared. The doors burst inward, and a strong wind burst from its maw knocking them both to the ground. Heat rolled from the dark beyond. Iyren stood and steadied himself at the threshold, drawn toward the void.

"Wait," she said again, more plea than command now. He glanced back at her. For an instant the old conflict flickered across his face, wanting to stay, needing to go. Then whatever he heard in that unlit space pulled harder. "I have to see it," he said.

All the arguments she had built on the walk here, every warning, every plea, every reminder of home, jammed in her throat. None of them could compete with the quiet certainty in his voice. She swallowed them down and forced out the only truth she had left. "Then... I'm going with you."

Iyren hesitated just long enough for her to see his eyes soften. Then he turned toward the dark and crossed the threshold. Veyra followed him into the ruin which swallowed them whole.

Crossing the threshold was like stepping into a mouth that had forgotten how to breathe. Sound dulled at once. The faint crackle from the ember bridge outside vanished as if someone had snapped closed a lid. Even their footsteps felt stolen, the soft scuff of their boots on the stone swallowed before it could echo.

Veyra's eyes strained against the dark. Ember-lit sconces lined the walls, spaced at regular intervals. Their flames burned with a steady, low orange glow but the jet stone drank in almost all of it. What should have been a warm glow became thin halos clinging close to each bowl, refusing to spread.

Beyond those frail circles, the corridors stretched away into suggestion and shadow. Iyren moved forward without hesitation. His shoulders were still hunched from the blast of the doors but his steps did not falter. He walked as if following a trail laid down long before he was born.

Veyra kept to his side, close enough that her sleeve brushed his. The contact steadied her more than the meagre light ever could. "This place isn't right," she whispered. "It doesn't have to be," he replied, eyes fixed ahead. "It only has to be true."

The words made no sense to her but he sounded so certain that arguing felt like throwing pebbles at a cliff face. The corridor twisted left, then right, then sharply left again. There were no markings on the stone. No carvings. No seams where blocks met. The ruin felt less built than grown, as if some single, enormous substance had set itself into these shapes and then chosen never to move again.

Occasionally, Veyra thought she saw movement at the edge of her vision, a flicker of shadow at a corridor's fork, a brief suggestion of a figure standing at the far end of a hall. Each time she turned her head, she found only empty stone and trembling ember-light.

"How do you know where to go?" she asked quietly.

His jaw tightened. "I do not."

"Then why are you walking like you do?" she said.

He hesitated, not in his stride but in his answer. "Because stopping feels worse."

They passed through an intersection where four corridors met. The air there held a faint tang of iron, like old blood washed too many times but never quite clean. Veyra's chest tightened. She glanced down and saw nothing but smooth, dark floor and the soft, faded footprints they left behind in the thin film of dust that had somehow found its way inside these sealed halls. There should not have been soot. But it was there, clinging to the edges of her soles, muting each step.

"You could still turn around," she murmured.

"You could," he said. "You know. I will not."

"I know." she said.

The corridor sloped downward so gradually. Veyra only noticed when her calves began to protest. The heat built with it. At first it felt like walking near a baker's oven, an old, steady warmth at the edge of tolerance. Then it grew heavier, pressing against their faces, weighing down each.

Sweat gathered at her temples and slid down her neck. Her shirt clung damply to her back. The air tasted faintly of charcoal and something she could not name, something that made her tongue feel strange in her mouth.

"Iyren..." she said, slowing without meaning to. "This isn't just heat. This is..."

"It is close," he said and there was a tremor in his voice now, not of fear but of nearness.

"We're almost there." She swallowed. "And what happens when we get there?"

He did not answer. His stride lengthened instead. They passed another sconce, its flame sat very low, barely more than a coal. As Iyren walked by, it flared higher for an instant, then settled again once he had gone. Veyra stared at it, heart pounding, then hurried after him.

The corridor opened at last into a broad antechamber. The heat hit her like a physical blow. Veyra staggered, dropping a hand to one knee to keep herself upright. The air here was thick and heavy, clinging to her skin like a second, burning cloak; it scorched her throat on the way in and sat in her lungs like hot stone.

Iyren straightened. Before them, the room stretched wide and high but the edges blurred behind a roiling shimmer. Embers glowed in narrow trenches along the walls but their light bent strangely, pulled inward toward the chamber's center where the heat was fiercest.

Veyra forced her head up, squinting against the wavering air. At first she thought it was just more distortion, a place where light bent wrong and refused to settle. Then the shape resolved, slowly, like something coming into focus behind thick glass. A single, enormous ember hung in the middle of the room.

It was not perched on any pedestal or bowl. It simply hovered there, suspended at chest height, its surface a deep, unnatural black. Veins of violet and sickly green pulsed beneath that darkness, like slow lightning trapped under stone. No flame licked from it. No tongues of fire danced. It was burning without burning, eating the space around it in a silent, steady consumption.

The light in the room lost colour the closer it drew to that core. Shadows bled toward it and disappeared. Iyren stared at it as if seeing something he had been waiting for since the first time he'd ever looked into a hearth. Veyra swallowed against the dryness in her throat.

"Iyren," she said hoarsely. "Do not go any closer." He took one step forward. "Iyren!"

Her voice broke. "Listen to me! Whatever that is, it is not meant for you."

He flinched, just slightly. Enough that she saw his shoulders twitch, his hand curl briefly into a fist at his side. He stood there for the span of a heartbeat, caught between her voice and whatever pressed at him from the ember. The pull won. He stepped forward. The world seemed to pause for a breath. Then it consumed him.

The chamber erupted in black-green light, soundless, absolute. When it cleared, Iyren stood at the heart of what remained. Flames that were not flames tore upward around him, strands of black shot through with violent colour, wrapping and unwrapping his body like molten cords. His clothes should have burned. His hair should have gone to soot. His skin should have blistered and split. None of it did. His lips moved but she heard no words.

Whatever conversation took place within that blaze did not need sound to exist. His face twisted, once in agony, once in rapture, once in something so raw she had no name for it. A laugh tore out of him. It cracked across the chamber like a fault line. Not wholly mad, not wholly sane. It sounded like a man who had been handed proof that everything he had feared and hoped in secret was true, and that the cost of knowing would peel him away from himself.

Veyra sobbed, though she did not remember choosing to. Tears cut lines through the dirt on her cheeks, she could feel the sting of the slash on her face. The light dulled slowly, shrinking back into the ember's core. The flames that had not been flames sank inward, leaving the chamber hazy and scorched but intact.

Veyra's muscles trembled as the crushing heat eased enough for her to push herself up onto her hands. Iyren stood where the ember had been. It was still there, she realised, dazedly, hovering just behind him, smaller now, its veins of colour beating slow and deep. But her eyes could not hold on it for long. They were drawn instead to him.

Soot streaked his face and arms in washed-out greys. Ash clung to his hair. His clothes looked much as they had before, only darker at the edges, as if the seams alone had been singed. But it was his eyes that stopped her. They were too clear. The fevered edge, the fractured uncertainty that had haunted him since he returned from the forest the first time, those were gone.

In their place sat a terrible calm. A certainty that did not bend. It was not the easy confidence of someone who knew how to light a fire in the rain. It was the cold, bright assurance of someone who believed he had just been shown the shape of the world's true order.

He looked at his hands as if seeing them for the first time. Slowly, he flexed his fingers. When he curled them into fists, faint motes of ember-light glowed beneath the skin, then faded. Veyra's stomach turned. "Iyren," she whispered. He turned toward her.

For a heartbeat, she thought, hoped, that the sight of her kneeling there, shaking, would break through whatever had settled over him. That he would run to her, apologize, collapse under the weight of what he'd done. Instead, he regarded her with something like tenderness and something like distance, both layered atop that frightening clarity.

"You'll see," he said softly. The words were almost gentle. "I'll show you."

Her vision blurred. The boy she'd followed was gone. What stood there now only wore his shape. Still, she rose from the ground and followed, because she could not let him walk alone. The ruin's warmth followed.

Chapter Nine

The cave held a slow pulse around her. Selura lay still and listened to the thrum in the stone, a sound she had trusted for years, now thinned at the edges like a knot rubbed too long. Dawn had not yet broken. The Homefire painted the walls in a low amber, and the colour made the rock seem closer than it was. Mira slept on her side. Bren sat propped against the wall, chin dipped, the kind of half sleep a stubborn watcher takes. Aravel checked a bowstring by touch rather than sight. The air carried a faint metallic taste from the river mouth.

She rose by degrees, careful with her weight. A tremor ran under her skin and then was gone, a quick thread that felt not wholly hers. When it passed, it left a quiet ache along her ribs. She sat until it settled.

Aravel saw the change and stood. He did not speak immediately. He weighed her stance, the colour in her face and the steadiness of her hands.

"You are up," he said. "How are you?"

"It has not settled," Selura said. "It pulls two ways. I do not know what happens if I push back."

"Can you walk?"

"I can walk," she said. "Though I do not know if I should."

The measured tap of Eshra's staff came from the darker part of the cavern bay. The elder set the staff by the wall and lowered herself to the floor. Her eyes were clear.

"It is not only Dream," Eshra said. "The land is thin. The cords are out of tune. Even the river has lost its centre note."

Aravel rubbed his jaw and listened to the quiet that followed. "Something is wrong in the Silver Forest."

A cold drift moved through the mouth of the cave and laid the taste of iron on Selura's tongue. It was familiar in a way that did not comfort, like the aftertaste of the first word spoken. She set her palm to the floor to take the stone's measure. The thrum wavered and steadied.

"We cannot stay," she said. "Sitting here longer just makes it worse."

"You can barely stand," Aravel said.

"I will stand enough," Selura said. "I need to see where the edge lies. I need to know whether pressing helps or tears it."

Eshra watched her without blinking. "If you go, you will pay," she said. "That place is not somewhere to be trifled with."

Selura's fingers tightened around her knee. "Then I will pay," she said. "If the forest gives way, the valley follows."

Aravel drew air once and let his shoulders set. "If you go, I go," he said. "You will not walk in there alone."

"You do not owe me anything Aravel," Selura said.

"I owe the valley," he said. "And I do not trust the wood with you unguarded."

Mira woke cleanly and pulled her cloak close against the chill. She looked at Selura first, then at Eshra, then toward the mouth of the cave. A thin draft crossed the stone and went still.

"Say the plan out loud," Mira said. "I need to hear it."

Selura did not rush the answer. She tasted the air again and chose words she could keep. "We walk to the edge," she said. "If it lets us, we take one step in. If it presses back, we stop. No argument after we set that rule."

"What else," Mira said.

"Knots at every stop," Eshra said. "They do not teach. They keep harm at the edge and they mark your way home."

Selura nodded. "If my voice thins or wanders, call it. If it will not steady, we turn back. No heroics."

"Agreed," Aravel said.

Bren pushed himself upright with a low sound and rolled one shoulder until it loosened. He checked the simple things first. Rope, a Waterskin and a small jar wrapped in cloth.

"I heard enough," he said. "I will carry the rope. If it comes to it, I will carry her too."

"You will not need to carry me," Selura said.

"You say that every time," Bren said, but there was a small smile in it that warmed the room without changing the fact.

Aravel looked toward the valley path. "Neri and Mara," he said. "If they will come, they take the sides. They are quickest on uneven ground."

Selura let those names settle. The tremor under her skin returned, sharper for a heartbeat and then thin again. She steadied herself with the stone until the line inside her held.

"I do not know what pushing will do," she said, and now her voice was low enough that it did not carry past this circle. "I do not know what I am bringing with me when I try. Staying still answers nothing."

Mira stepped close and set a hand on her arm. "First light," she said. "Eat something. Pack simple. Knots at every stop. If you say we turn, we turn."

Eshra leaned forward and ran a finger along a shallow groove in the floor. "When you leave, leave this room in order," she said. "Set the Homefire safe. Put the gear back to the wall. This place has held you. Let it keep its shape."

Selura looked at each of them in turn. Aravel, steady as a post set deep. Mira, fierce and exact. Bren, unshaken in the work of carrying. Eshra, watchful enough for all of them. Beyond them, the thought of Neri and Mara like two quick notes waiting to be called. They were gathering not by order but by need, as the valley always had when winter pressed early.

She rose carefully. Her balance dipped, then steadied. Aravel's hand came under her elbow until she found her balance, then he let go without being asked.

"Easy," he said.

"I will not break, it is alright." Selura said.

"I believe you," Aravel said. "But you still will not carry it alone."

They moved without hurry. Aravel fixed his bow and checked the heads in his quiver. Bren tied the rope to his pack in a way that would spill clean if pulled fast. Mira split a strip of dried meat, handed half to Selura, and tucked the rest into Bren's pack.

"Wake the others," Selura said. "It is time; the forest awaits."

They stood a moment longer and listened. Coals shifted in the Homefire and set a soft rhythm. Outside, the river held to the wrong pitch, as if a string had slipped and would not tune.

The ruin kept its own weather. Heat lay in the halls as if the jet echoed the essence of fire. Iyren and Veyra climbed the inner stair, their boots on the steps the only sound that carried. A torch on the landing sank to a wisp of flame when Iyren drew near, then steadied after he passed.

They stepped out to the high balcony of jet, its rail missing in wide bites and the floor laced with fine cracks. Veyra welcomed the cool; Iyren showed no change. At the ruin's flank the chasm dropped until sight failed. Beyond it the Silver Forest lay like a vast sea. The canopy caught the strange light and glistened like starlight. Here and there new forms showed where none were marked before: rings of pale stone set among the trunks, shards of jet that rose like teeth, and a long straight gap where nothing grew, the earth scraped clean.

Veyra turned to speak and stopped. The torch in her hand leaned from Iyren and thinned. A fresh silver thread showed at his temple and the skin at the corner of his eye had drawn tight. Heat came off him in a dry wave and yet he did not seem to feel it. She shifted the torch farther from his shoulder and said nothing.

They kept to the balcony's run until it opened on the broken court. Columns rose like ribs. The floor had split and heaved long ago and never found itself again. Iyren knelt at a fault and held his palm above it. Darkfire answered. It curled to his call in a thread of black with violet and a thin green that walked the edges. The heat it gave was sharp and dry. Where it kissed the rim of the crack the jet did not char; it softened and slumped, like stone under acid. Mortar hissed and ran in thin streams. Other flame near it drew smaller as if pressed. The crack widened by a finger. Dust lifted, then fell straight, as if the air would not keep it. Veyra watched the green rim, took its measure and still did not speak.

Veyra stepped back. "You draw too hard."

Iyren shut his hand. The thread pinched to a point and went out. "It is not hard. It is precise."

"Precise still takes from something." She looked past him to the forest.

Sure enough, small changes set in while he worked. Another silver thread marked his temple, the lines at his mouth set deeper and the skin at his eye drew fine and did not fully return. Simple things one may not notice unless looking carefully.

"Veyra," he said. "When we were younger, did you listen for where the river thins before it turns."

"I listened for where it eats the bank," she said. "We were not from gentle water."

"There is a thinning in the forest," Iyren said. "Not a bend. It feels as if the bank is no longer there."

They left the court for the lower galleries. At a niche where roots had pushed in, Iyren crouched. The roots were pale and dry, not dead, held in a pause that felt worse. He reached without calling the flame. Wood powdered under his thumb.

Veyra watched his face. "How long since you slept."

"I do not know." He wiped the dust from his fingers. "Sleep does not help me find what I need."

"What do you need," she asked.

He did not answer. The air pressed close against the jet around them, and even the heat made no sound. What should have echoed simply died against the walls.

In that quiet he understood what the ruin had been built to deny. The beauty he had worshipped was only rot that wore the shape of life. Dream's endless making was no mercy. It only fed the wound. Darkfire was the answer. It cut clean. It stilled.

He turned toward the passage ahead. "We go to the meadow," he said. "It began there. It will end there."

Veyra stared at him. "You cannot mean to start the fires again."

"I mean to finish what was begun."

She took a step closer, searching his face. "Iyren, that nearly killed us the first time. You think ending is mercy, but this; this isn't you."

He looked past her toward the narrow hall. "It is now."

Iyren turned his hand palm up. A small sphere formed, the same dark thread, and it drew a narrow ring of colour out of the air around it. The torch behind them shrank as if a larger shadow had crossed it. A new silver line showed at his temple, fine as a hair. He closed his hand. The ring took a moment to fade.

"I am not choosing an end," he said. "I am choosing a path through what is already ending."

She looked at his hand, at the faint shimmer where the ring had been, then at the thin silver line cutting through his temple. For a long while she said nothing. The heat from the jet walls pressed close, dull and heavy. When she finally spoke, her voice had lost its edge.

"Then I suppose we walk," she said. "There's nothing left here to wait for."

He almost smiled. "Agreed."

They gathered what they would carry. Veyra packed what still had meaning to her: a skin of water, a shard of polished jet for cutting, a strip of dried root to stave hunger. Iyren carried nothing that needed hands. The heat that lingered in him was enough. At the stair, Veyra paused and touched the knot at her wrist. She had tied it for luck when she was young and too proud to ask for more. The cord rasped under her fingers. The small knot held its shape.

They left the ruin by the west gate where the air opened into the chasm. The ember bridge waited, low and steady, its surface dim but alive. They crossed in silence. When their boots met the jet platform on the far side, the bridge crackled and hissed, burning itself out until nothing remained above the gap.

Ahead, the forest rose from the slope, the silver canopy shifting in slow, uneven waves. What had looked still from the balcony now carried its own quiet motion, branches folding and unfolding as if testing the air.

They stepped from the jet lip onto cool soil. The first ranks of trunks stood close, no space wide enough for two to pass together. The leaves above held their silver without shimmer. When they turned, the veins caught a brief violet glint and went still again.

Iyren moved first. Behind them, the gap lay dark and clean, the bridge gone.

Veyra looked back once, then followed him into the trees. Somewhere ahead, the ground darkened. Iyren did not search for it with his eyes. He walked toward the place where the map in his mind had already run out.

They went deeper.

Morning reached the valley in copper and blue, the river carrying both as it turned below.

Selura stepped out first, stilling herself before the day began. Mira followed, half-awake, Bren rubbing at his face as he joined them. Aravel was already at the boundary markers, testing the new stakes with the habit of someone who needs to be sure.

Seyra and Eshra waited nearby, their hands already moving as they braided the final strands of cord. The work looked simple, but every turn carried its own pattern. The first knot hung between them, broad and steady, holding the unspoken weight of parting.

Seyra glanced up. "You took your time."

Selura smiled faintly. "We were gathering what we still need."

"There's never enough time for that," Eshra said. "But the morning gives what it can."

Selura joined them at the boundary and touched the new cord. The tone that answered was uneven, a wavering sound beneath her palm.

"It feels off," Mira said.

"It is," Seyra replied. "Dream's rhythm changes when the world does. That's why these knots matter now."

Seyra handed Selura a length of cord, still warm from use and carrying the faint scent of the herbs the elders used to sharpen focus. Selura looped it once around her fingers, the pattern returning as if she had never stopped.

"Show them," Seyra said.

Selura knelt and tied a single knot at the base of the marker. The motion was quick and sure. When it settled, a pulse of calm moved through her chest and stayed.

Eshra nodded. "That will hold."

Aravel came next, his knot plain and directional, a mark to guide rather than call. Mira followed with a tighter hand but strong intent, and Bren after her, trying not to copy Seyra's grip and doing it anyway. The cord took all of it, quiet and enduring.

Seyra looked over their work. "Leave one at each place you rest," she said. "And another wherever the air feels thin."

Mira asked, "The forest paths; will they listen?"

Eshra paused. "No one knows what listens there," she said. "Still, the knots should hold as they always have. They mark your way home."

Risa appeared from the dens, arms wrapped around herself, her face pale from a restless night. She stopped behind Mira until Selura turned and beckoned her forward.

"You're leaving again," the girl whispered.

"Only for a while," Selura said.

"The forest hurt you last time."

Selura rested a hand on her cheek. "I'll be careful."

Risa looked toward the cord. "May I tie one?"

Seyra hesitated, then offered her a short length. "Go on. A child's knot remembers what grown hands forget."

The girl worked slowly, tongue caught between her teeth. The knot came out crooked but firm. When she pulled it tight, the whole line gave a brief tremor and then stilled.

Eshra smiled. "That one will last."

A quick step sounded on the path. Daran arrived with his spear, breath sharp from running.

"Let me come," he said. "I can help."

Aravel shook his head. "The valley needs watchers."

"I can fight."

"You can learn," Aravel said, steady but not unkind. "Today you watch."

The boy turned to Selura. "If something comes while you're gone?"

"Then keep them safe," she said. "That's what you took the spear for."

He swallowed the answer he wanted to give and settled on a single nod.

Seyra pulled the last knot tight. "There. The line's ready."

Selura looked over the band: Aravel steady, Mira already testing the wind, Bren calm and watchful. A little apart, Neri and Mara packed in silence. Six now, and for the first time it felt complete.

She pressed her palm to the first knot. "Thank you," she said, to the elders and to the craft that would hold behind them.
Eshra touched her shoulder. "Walk with care."

Seyra added, "Return with what you learn."

Selura drew a slow breath and faced her companions. "We go."

They passed through the boundary. Each knot gave a faint shimmer as she went by, one after another, leading toward the Silver Forest. Children watched from the dens, whispering. Some reached toward the cords and let their hands fall back.

Risa stayed near her knot. "Will it remember me?"

"It already does," Selura said. She guided the girl's fingers back to it. "Anything made with care keeps its place."

Daran lingered near the elders, spear low. "When the valley hears your names, it will know who stayed," he said, not quite loudly enough to call it pride.

Eshra pressed a carved charm into his hand; river runes cut along its face. "Then watch well. The watchers matter as much as those who go."

He nodded, jaw tight, and slipped the charm against his chest.

When the final knot settled, the line gave a single, steady tone; neither bright nor dark, only true. The travellers gathered at the mouth of the valley.

"If we do not return," Selura said.

Eshra answered, "Then the world will know you meant to."

Selura bowed once, turned, and led them toward the trees. The others followed, not by order but by need, into the shade beyond the valley.

While morning spread through the valley, its colour struck the Silver Forest in a different way. Iyren and Veyra moved beneath trees that rose like pillars through a restless gleam. The air held a strange weight, thick with the quiet sounds of living things unseen. The leaves above clattered like metal, their veins flashing violet before the canopy settled back into shade.

Veyra lifted her torch and watched the silver leaves stir. "The forest's calm never lasts," she said.

Iyren did not answer. The change met him as soon as they crossed the shade line. Dream's trace thinned and withdrew like a tide leaving shore. In the quiet it left behind, another weight settled; a steady pressure at the back of his thoughts, patient and certain.

They followed a narrow run where the forest floor had thinned. Patches of black earth showed through the piles of leaves. The air was still, and the smell that came from the soil was sharp, like iron left too long in water. Veyra crouched and pressed her fingers into one of the darker places. The dirt broke apart under her touch, fine and dry, as if something had eaten the bind from it.

She straightened slowly. "This is wrong."

Iyren looked past her to where the roots rose in knotted seams. The same wrongness stirred in him, but it felt clean, deliberate. "The forest is changing," he said.

Veyra shook her head. "Changing into what."

He studied the blackened soil, the way it seemed to breathe. "Into what it was meant to be."

A dark thread stirred at the edge of his sight and bent the air slightly. He did not take it yet. He walked on.

Deeper in, the trunks drew close and colour fell to blue grey. The way split around a long cavity cut through the ground, a gouge deeper than the roots. Veyra slowed. "We should go around."

Iyren stepped down into the cut and stilled. "Wait."

The ground shivered. A distortion wavered at the far end of the run, blurring the roots and the space between them. The air grew dense and bent, as if the world there were being pulled toward itself. Out of that strain, a figure began to glide forward, half within the air and half within its own reflection. A Nymire moved between the trees, drifting closer in its search for what still lived.

It was half made, part flesh and part absence, shifting as the eye tried to fix it. A ribcage showed through a frame of bone and rot, the skin half-formed and sliding away in slow motion. It glided inches above the ground, a wet gargle rising from its throat as it choked on the Dream it fed from. Ragged black cloth clung to it in strips, shifting with each motion, and its long skeletal hands dragged the air as it passed, claws catching light like wet glass. Where it went, colour dulled and a stench of rot spread, the forest seeming to recoil from its hunger.

Veyra's chest locked.

Iyren raised his hand.

Dark fire answered in a narrow ribbon, black and violet coiling with a thin sickly green along its edge. The flame struck the Nymire mid-glide. The creature recoiled as if struck from within, letting out a horrible shrill shriek that tore through the stillness and rattled the air around them. The ground beneath it blackened, then bleached to a dead grey. The space between them warped, fire and flesh bending away from each other in violent recoil. The Nymire shuddered, its form flickering in and out of shape before it turned and slid into the dark between the trunks, leaving the stench of rot behind. Iyren lowered his hand. The air steadied. A fine tremor ran across his fingers and then stopped.

Veyra stood at the edge of the scorched ring. The heat still wavered across it, faint and uneven. Iyren's hand hung open at his side, the last threads of fire curling away. The forest seemed to hold its distance, sound pressed flat.

She looked at him. "You drove it off."

He did not answer. The silver at his temple caught the movement of the air, bright for an instant and then gone.

Her voice came lower. "Selura gave everything to do what you just did."

Iyren's gaze stayed fixed on the dark between the trunks where the Nymire had slipped away. "She prayed to a voice that took more than it ever gave."

The stillness between them deepened. Veyra's pulse still hammered from the fight, yet the sight of him, steady and untouched, pulled at her. She took a step closer, then another, until the warmth from the ring reached her boots. For a heartbeat she hesitated. Then she crossed it and fell in beside him.

Iyren's mind held fragments of the thing that had called him. Not a voice. A pattern. Heat above stone. A river turned to glass. A figure the colour of ash. A face he knew, rippled and split. He could not tell whether it came from the same dark that fed his fire or from something older still, waiting beneath it.

Veyra kept her voice even. "What will be left when you finish?"

Iyren's eyes stayed on the horizon. "A world that stops moving," he said. "One that can rest and stay as it was meant to."

They moved on. Behind them, the ruin sank into shadow, its black walls swallowing what little light remained. The forest pressed close, silent and waiting. Iyren walked as if drawn by a current beneath the soil, and Veyra kept beside him, the heat at their backs fading to nothing. Ahead, the ground tilted downward, pulling them toward purpose.

Near nightfall, darkness gathered in the sky and streaks of vibrant aurora: greens, violets, pinks, and reds stretched across the expanse; an omen. The stars, normally energetic and poised to move, held their place waiting in witness. The dome of the world drew tight as if the making beneath it all strained for one last turn.

High above the ground below, the canopy gave a metallic clatter and then stilled. The sounds of the unseen eased, and the dark crept in.

Mara moved ahead, quick on her feet, wiry with a close-cut braid at her neck. Neri ranged opposite with her bow at half draw, long-limbed, hair bound tight, eyes steady. Aravel kept the centre with Selura and watched the small tremor that ran through her hand.

"We are too deep already," Mira said.

"I feel it too," Selura said. "We go together to the next sure ground and mark it, then we can decide our next move."

Unbeknownst to the band, they had just reached a clearing where Iyren had once stood. At its centre a giant trunk had folded in on itself, a crown of wood collapsed and turned inward. From some angles the ridges and hollows gathered into the suggestion of eyes and a mouth, as if a face had been taken apart and set back wrong. Veins that once ran violet were black and split. Sap had dried to a dark gloss; plates of bark had sloughed and lay curled at the roots.

Around it stood the silver seams; tall, near-vertical rifts that opened and narrowed without wind. Their edges shone like cut metal. When one widened, a thin layered tone came from within and a colour none could describe. The ground near them showed long bleached streaks, then charcoal patches, then places rubbed to powder.

Selura set her palm to the ruined bark. A weak current rose under her skin, raw and uneven, and snapped back. The sight matched what had come to her in dreams: a seam opening and a black corruption sliding through.

Aravel stepped in and set a hand on her forearm. "Easy," he said. "We do not know what that is, it could be dangerous."

Selura nodded once, shock still in her face. "I know the shape," she said quietly. "I have seen it before. Not here, but I have seen it."

From the clearing of the speaking tree they kept a measured pace into harder ground. The ground changed from soft litter to a brittle crust that cracked at a step. Roots arched high where the topsoil had worn away. A bitter metal tang rode under the sweet of rot. They spoke only to work the way forward: "Watch that step," "that way," "hold." At a firm stump they tied one quick knot and moved on.

The trees opened by degrees and stone began to show. Low shelves and narrow ledges that asked for care. Aravel tested each edge with the end of his spear and chose the crossing. Neri pointed a tight gap between two rocks and waited until Selura saw it. Mara took a short ledge to the right and showed an open palm to guide them through. Twice they turned when the surface crumbled under a boot. Selura kept them close; the tremor in her hand did not leave.

At last, the wood thinned enough to show the shape ahead. Stone ribs ringed a broad depression; the floor below lay scoured bare in long arcs. They held to cover at the rim and took its measure.

Far ahead of the band Iyren and Veyra reached the forest's core, a dark interval where trees thinned and stone took over: stacked rock faces with a dull sheen and narrow ridges. The floor was scraped to bare earth in places, rutted elsewhere, and pocked with patches that crumbled to powder under a boot. Iyren moved on a map only he could feel. Veyra matched him, eyes on the rock edges.

Veyra studied him. "Hold a moment. There is more silver in your hair than there was on the ridge."

"It is not sickness," he said. "It is direction. Some payment must be expected."

They stood on the rim of the great depression before them. On the far rim, Selura's band stepped out and stopped. Selura cut her hand low to halt them and called across the distance. "Iyren!"

"You should have stayed in the valley!" he called back.

Selura started them down the slope in single file, careful on the ledges. Iyren and Veyra did the same working along a shelf that angled toward the centre. They closed the distance by degrees until the two groups faced each other across fifteen paces of scraped ground.

"We need to cross," Selura said. "We will keep to our line and move on."

Iyren turned his palm.

A bar of dark fire leapt from rock to rock two strides ahead of her band and held, black at the core, violet and green walking its rim. Heat pressed against their shins, dry and absolute.

"Not here," he said. "Not past me."

Selura did not test it. "Iyren, look at me. We are not here to fight you. We came to stop what's poisoning this place."

"You can not cure what's already becoming," he said. "Dream's order failed. This is what comes after."

Aravel stepped forward, spear grounded. "You're feeding the same rot you claim to fight."

Iyren's gaze sharpened. "I'm cleansing what Dream left to fester."

Selura shook her head. "You're burning what's left alive."

He raised his hand, and the fire line flared. "Better burned clean than left to choke."

A silence hung. The band stood just outside the heat. Selura's eyes caught the faint silver at his temple, the hollows deepening at his cheeks. "This isn't you," she said softly. "Whatever calls you isn't mercy."

"It is truth," Iyren said. "And truth doesn't ask permission."

The words settled heavy between them.

Then, from below the rocks, came a wet rasp. Then another. Then many.

Shapes slid out of the basin, gliding inches above the ground, edges flickering like bad reflection. The stench came first: sweet, wet, and wrong. A fallen limb near the shelf sagged and went slack as one passed.

"Form!" Aravel said. "Neri high, Mara with her! Bren on me! Mira get to Selura!"

Iyren set his stance. Veyra shifted clear of his arm.

The first Nymire lunged. Iyren cut tight. The flame met it mid-glide; the creature recoiled as if struck from within and let out a shrill, tearing cry. It slid aside. Another filled the gap. Fine silver laddered farther from Iyren's eye; his hair dulled by a shade. His hand shook once, then steadied inside the heat. He fired again.

"Two right," Neri called. "One high, one low."

"I have the low," Aravel said. His spear found weight and broke a thin torso. A second shape grazed his shoulder with a claw that barely touched him and still opened skin leaving withered skin around the wound.

Mira dragged Bren back a step and shoved his knife into his palm. "Hold here."

Selura drew once. The knots at her belt answered; a white force climbed her arm, alive and sharp. It gathered at her palm and broke forward in a single pane of white. Pain traced up the side of her face, a thin red line under her nose. "Back two," she said, and the blast struck.

The nearest three Nymire wavered and bent backward as if the air around them had turned solid, their outline thinning before dissolving in the presence of Dream's power. Veyra touched Iyren's sleeve and flinched at the heat. "Left side. One thin, one whole."

"I see them." He turned and let loose. The thin one recoiled and turned its gaze; the whole one slipped through the space it left focusing again on Iyren.

"More coming!" Aravel yelled.

Roots lifted as if something beneath had turned. Their ring shrank a step.

"Mara, mark the ground!" he continued.

Mara's knot flared and held a boundary for three hard beats. "Marked." The flare broke. Bren's knife hand slipped in the chaos, the weight of the recoil driving him half back. Mira caught his shoulder and steadied him with both hands. "Get up!" she said. He nodded once, jaw tight, and reset his stance.

Iyren swept his hand. Fire ran wide, black at the centre with faint violet walking the rim. The trunks near the blast bowed inward, drawn by some unseen gravity. Iyren looked older now—silver seams deep at the corners of his eyes, his skin drawn taut across bone. Still he raised his hand again, voice low. "Not yet."

"Stay tight," Selura said, voice steady only by will. "No clear lanes."

The ground heaved beneath them. Roots lifted, soil cracking open in long seams. The air thickened until it felt like wading through water.

From the rim came movement, many shapes, not one. The trees bent as if pushed by a rising tide. Dozens of dark cloaked figured slid between the far trunks, each half-made and devouring what held it together. The air thickened with the wet sound of feeding. Rot spread faster than the eye could track.

Selura dropped to one knee. Aravel's spear slipped. Bren's knife arm hung useless. For every Nymire that fell, two more pressed through. The dark pulsed with their hunger.

Veyra's torch went out. Mira whispered a name no one caught.

They were surrounded now, edges closing, shapes folding together until the forest itself began to crawl. The noise of the groaning and choking overwhelmed the scene.

Selura found Iyren's eyes. "Iyren…"

Chapter Ten

Iyren's world hung inside that single moment, a heartbeat stretched too long to belong to any living thing. Sound fell away until the only noise that remained was the quiet beat inside his chest. The wet rasp of Nymire throats, the scrape of claws through bark and bone, the cries of those who fought beside him all slowed until they felt distant and thin. What pressed against his thoughts was not silence, but a waiting shape, a presence that filled every gap inside him.

It reached for him in waves, patient and vast, moving through the sparsely treed basin without sound. It wanted a door. It wanted him. He could feel it sliding against the walls of his mind, finding every crack he had tried to hide. For an instant he thought it might pass him by, that he might still refuse it. Then anger rose, familiar and safe. The anger had a weight that he let build until it filled his chest. The thing pressing at him did not retreat; it only folded into that anger, sharpening it.

He thought of the valley, of the people who had called his name and turned away when they saw what he had become. He thought of Selura's eyes when she told him to stand down and of the knots shivering under her hands as the Nymire broke through. He thought of everything he had ever built being ground to soil, of every word left unsaid. He could almost hear the old songs the elders had sung about cleansing fires, about the way ash gave the world a second chance. If there was mercy left, it was buried too deep to reach.

The presence pressed harder. He did not fight it this time. He let it draw closer until the edge of himself began to blur. The thought came clear and final: there was nothing left worth saving. If the world would not bend, then it would burn. He felt his heartbeat again, but it no longer belonged to him. Each pulse seemed to strike through stone.

Burn it clean.

The force formed without effort. The moment it existed inside him, the world seemed to shift. The air folded inward, drawn to him. Heat rose from the ground, threading through his legs and spine. For a heartbeat he thought the sky had fallen, but it was light, violent and wrong, pouring from his skin. It began at the center of his chest, a deep shadowed violet that ran outward along his veins. Black lines followed, twisting and splitting into patterns that no human hand could make. Green light followed them, chasing each line like new growth racing through cracks in stone. The sensation was neither pain nor relief; it was recognition. Something old had finally been allowed to move.

The ground answered first. Soil cracked open in rings around his feet. The air bent, then broke. A roar filled the basin; not sound exactly, more the force of something too large to be contained. It struck outward. The first wave threw the nearest Nymire from their feet. They hit the ground in broken shapes, writhing and screeching in the burn of the dark flame. The second wave shattered great trees that had once stood as a strength against the backdrop of the ever-darkening wood. The third reached the far rim of the clearing, ripping through the fog until daylight burst through in ragged bands.

Iyren's body was lost inside it. His vision scattered, and when it steadied again he was standing in a storm of his own making. The streams of shadowed fire poured from his skin in long spirals. Every movement carried a trail of burning colour behind it; vibrant greens and violets. His fingers no longer looked like fingers. They glowed from the inside, as if their bones turned to luminous glass. The ground under him was molten earth that refused to swallow him. He felt no heat. The fire belonged to him; the world simply suffered for it.

Shapes rushed at him from the smoke. Nymire in their hundreds, drawn by the essence of Dream all around him. He turned his gaze upon them, and they broke apart. No gesture, no word, only the will behind his eyes. They fell, screeching and collapsing, parts of their bodies coming apart in plumes that joined the storm. The forest answered their fall. Roots lifted from the soil, trunks splitting lengthwise. The ground breathed a dark fire that consumed the light. It climbed through the roots, racing along the forest floor. The blaze spread outward in circles, each pulse feeding the next.

Selura was at the edge of it, still standing though the blast had knocked the others to the ground. Her hair had come loose; her face streaked with ash. She lifted a hand toward him, but the air between them rippled with force; the protective shimmer of Dream. She did not call to him; she only raised her hand as if to remember who he was. The shimmer widened for an instant, enough to shield the few who still lived near her. It held just long enough for the wave to pass.

The area around him convulsed. Stone split beneath his feet. The sound tore the air in half. Iyren could feel the presence surging through him, spilling through every fracture. It no longer felt separate. It was him now; the will, the motion, the heat that demanded more. He could sense its satisfaction in the way the fire curved around his body, feeding and rising. The Nymire had been pushed back and decimated, but the forest still burned. Every root seemed to carry the fire deeper, spreading it through soil. It would reach the valley soon. He felt the knowledge like a promise.

He tried to remember the first time he had felt this power, when it had been only a whisper at the edge of sleep. He had thought then that it was mercy, that the world had chosen him to make things right. Now he understood that mercy had never been the point. The world did not want saving. It wanted ending. His hands trembled, not from fear but from release. The fire within him wanted to move again, and he could not tell if he was the one commanding it or if it had already decided.

He turned his head toward the forest's far edge. The path to the river lay somewhere beyond the smoke. The sky had gone the colour of burnt metal. Branches collapsed in slow motion, sending sparks in drifting arcs. The heat distorted everything. For a moment he thought he saw figures moving inside the fire, faces in the haze of heat, memories in the flame. They leaned toward him, pleading, but their voices were drowned in the noise of the world coming apart.

Something deep within the earth gave way. The blast's echo rolled back through the basin, driving ash upward in a storm that blotted out the last trace of daylight. When the ash settled, Iyren stood alone. His eyes reflected the strange green light that still twisted through the clearing. His expression did not change. Whatever had lived in him before was gone. In its place was only the quiet certainty that the work had begun and would not stop.

At the outer ring of the ruin, Selura rose. Her shield flickered once more before fading to a faint shimmer that clung to her skin. She could still see him through the haze, a figure made of fire and shadow, unmoving at the center. She whispered his name, but the wind carried it away. The ground trembled again. Then came silence. Iyren did not look back.

The dark light that poured from Iyren began to fade, though the colour of it clung to his skin. His face had taken on a mirrored sheen, the surface of his eyes turned pale silver as if reflecting something no one else could see. Each step he took left a faint glow where his feet met the scorched ground. The air around him quivered with heat, but the fire no longer spread outward. It circled him instead, tracing his movements like a living boundary.

He looked upon the ruin he had made and felt no triumph. Only a stillness that was almost calm. The noise of the dying forest fell away until only the faint hiss of burning roots remained. Behind him, the surviving band of the valley stirred; broken, coughing, their voices faint. He turned once, enough to see them through the smoke, then looked beyond them to the path leading east. The river's pull was a thread in his mind, distant but relentless. It felt like purpose.

"Dream failed," he said. The words came hollow and metallic, as though spoken from deep within a cave. "It watched and waited and did nothing. I will finish what it would not."

His voice reached the far edge of the clearing, carried on the fire's heat. Veyra was the first to move toward him. Her face was grey with soot; her hair matted to her skin. She stumbled once, then steadied herself. When she spoke, her voice broke halfway through his name. "Iyren; stop, there is nothing left to burn. Please."

He did not stop. He turned his head enough for her to see his face and the silver sheen that lived behind his eyes. It was not recognition that passed there, but indifference. The fire bent toward him with each step he took, answering to his movement as though drawn by command. "Go back," he said quietly. "This is not your path."

She shook her head but her feet would not move closer. The heat had grown too fierce. Between them the ground still smoldered, cracked and uneven. Each fissure pulsed with faint green light. She could smell the soil burning beneath it.

Behind her, Selura stirred. The shimmer that had shielded her was fading, its last threads evaporating into the haze. She pressed a hand to the ground and pushed herself upright. Blood streaked her cheek; her eyes were unfocused but searching.

The others began to gather, silent, circling around Selura as if instinct demanded they protect her. Ash drifted through the clearing in slow spirals, thickening into a storm that made it hard to tell what was living and what had already burned. Somewhere beyond the haze came the low clicking of movement. Nymire remnants, not yet destroyed, crawling out of the wreckage. Their shapes were twisted and uncertain, half melted by the blast, though still relentless, enduring and hungry, seeking the sustenance that sustained them.

Iyren's attention flicked toward the sound. The faintest shadow of a smile touched his mouth. He turned away from the survivors, stepping onto the path that led over the lip of the great depression and downhill through the shattered burning trees. Each gust of wind fanned the embers to life for an instant, the green and violet glow pulsing in its influence.

Veyra called to him one last time, her voice small against the rising wind. "Iyren, please. Do not go."

He did not answer. The fire coiled upward behind him as he moved, a serpentine wake that stretched toward the horizon. Beyond the ruin the path opened into a field of blackened stumps and molten rock. The river's glint showed faintly through the fog ahead. He kept walking toward it, steady, unhurried, each step erasing what little light remained around him.

Selura's hand closed around one of the fallen knots lying near her feet. Its strands were scorched, withered and lifeless, its life long gone, but she held it anyway as if the motion itself could keep her steady. Around her the others waited, watching the place where Iyren had disappeared. The ash began to settle. The first crack of distant thunder echoed from somewhere above the horizon, a sound more like the world taking its first breath than a storm beginning. None of them moved.

The slope leveled along Iyren's path. The burned trees thinned and the river's shimmer broke faintly through the fog; his pace never slowed. The air ahead of him shimmered with rising heat, a wavering curtain that distorted the world into bands of dull green and black. Each step pressed deeper into ash that gave beneath his feet like sand. His body no longer felt weight. The glow inside his skin had dulled, but the pressure of it remained; a restless pulse that demanded more.

A shape appeared ahead of him on the path. Selura stood between two half-burned trunks, her body a dark outline against the haze. The faint shimmer of Dream clung to her still, a ghost-light that caught the ash drifting through the air. Her hair was matted, the flecks in her eyes ran dull but she did not move aside. She had no weapon in her hands. Only the steadiness of someone who had already accepted what would happen next.

Iyren stopped several paces from her. The ground beneath him still steamed. For a moment neither spoke. The air pressed hard between them, thick with heat and the smell of charred roots. When he finally spoke, his voice was low and even. "Move, Selura. This path is not yours."

She shook her head, though her body trembled. "You have done enough. There is nothing left to cleanse."

He stepped forward once. The glow inside him surged at the sound of her voice, answering with a pulse of light through the cracks in his skin. "You think this was ever about enough." He lifted his hand. The air bent around it, a dark coil forming above his palm. It writhed like smoke made solid, colours twisting in and out of each other until it settled into something too dense to be flame. "It ends when it is finished. Not before."

Selura's eyes followed the coil but did not look away. "You are not ending anything. You are feeding what broke you." Her voice wavered, but the words did not. She took a step toward him, her boots sinking in the ash. "Dream is not gone. You have just stopped listening."

The words struck him harder than she could have known. His expression tightened. The hand holding the darkfire curled inward, the light around it dimming. For a heartbeat she thought he might stop. Then the power flared again, more violent, spilling through his fingers and crawling up his arm in branching lines. "Dream watched this world rot," he said. "It gave us hope and called it mercy. Mercy does not save anything."

Selura kept moving forward. She could feel the ground giving under each step and could smell the scorched minerals of the soil. The heat made her vision swim. Her body wanted to turn away, but she forced herself to hold his gaze. "Mercy is not meant to save," she said softly. "It is meant to remember."

The distance between them closed to less than ten paces. The glow from his body illuminated her face, turning her skin the colour of dawn before the sun breaks the horizon. The light was beautiful and terrible. She lifted her hand, palm outward. "If you keep walking, you will destroy what is left of us. And yourself."

He almost smiled, a thin curve of the mouth. "There is nothing left of me to destroy."

The ground shuddered beneath them. From the forest's edge came the rustle of movement; soft, deliberate. The remaining Nymire had begun to creep in, their eyes faintly red in the smoke. Their bodies moved with strange caution now, as if uncertain of their maker's intent. They came in uneven lines, dragging limbs that hissed as they touched the cooling earth.

Selura turned her head slightly, enough to see them gathering at the fringe of the ruined wood. "They are coming again," she whispered.

Iyren's gaze followed hers, then returned to her face. "Then step aside."

She did not move. "No."

The refusal landed between them like a blow. The darkfire above his palm writhed, drawing itself into a tighter coil. The air between them began to warp, the heat pulling the smoke into narrow spirals. Selura felt the first threads of Dream stir beneath her skin, the flecks in her eyes finding a new light against the dark, an ache more than a power. It wanted to reach for him, to stop what was about to happen, but she held it back. The choice had to be his.

The trees around them groaned as another section of the forest collapsed. Ash fell in thick sheets, coating their hair and shoulders. The Nymire crept closer, slow but relentless, their steps leaving faint trails of steam in the cooling ground. The sound of their movement filled the air; low, wet, constant.

Iyren's arm rose higher. The light leaking from his body grew until it stained the haze a pale green. "You will die for this," he said quietly.

Selura took another step forward. The glow of Dream flickered behind her eyes. "Then it will have meaning."

The power between them swelled, pressure without sound. The forest seemed to hold its breath. For a heartbeat everything stilled; the ash, the fire, even the air. Then the first Nymire lunged through the fog.

Selura stood rooted to the path. The Nymire's charge faltered when the ground broke beneath them, the world itself seeming to hesitate. Iyren's hand still burned with the dark coil that twisted above his palm. The smoke swirled between them, carrying the scent of ash and iron. For a moment it felt as if the earth had stopped moving, caught between two opposing forces that refused to yield.

The first Nymire reached her. Its limbs dragged furrows through the ash as it came on, but Selura did not step aside. She felt the faint shimmer within her rise, the same quiet resonance she had known since she first called Dream as a child. It was weaker now, thinned by exhaustion and grief, but it was there. It met the shadow rising from Iyren and held against it, fragile as glass.

He shouted her name. She barely heard it. The sound of his voice came distorted, stretched thin by the pressure building in the air. Her body trembled with the effort to keep standing. She could feel Dream gathering behind her ribs, an ache so deep it bordered on pain. It wanted release. It wanted through.

The Nymire lunged again. She let go.

Dream moved like water through stone; slow at first, then unstoppable. The force around her body flared into a sudden brightness that cut through the fog. Light poured outward, clear and cold, spreading through the basin in layered rings. It carried the scent of rain and distant rivers. The air shifted, charged, and the world bent beneath it.

The Nymire screamed. Their bodies, once dark and slick, became translucent. They unraveled as the light passed over them, dissolving into a fine mist that vanished as quickly as it formed. Every sound in the clearing rose into one great cry; the death of creatures and the birth of something older. The ground rippled outward. Trees bowed and then snapped, their trunks splitting from within. The forest's voice deepened into a groan that came from the roots themselves.

Iyren staggered backward. The fire in his hand flickered, faltered. The glow inside him fought against the light pouring from her, but the balance had shifted. The power he carried turned inward, no longer answering to his command. He tried to speak her name again, but his throat refused the sound. His body shook, light bleeding from every pore. For the first time, he looked afraid.

The force between them met and folded together, light and shadow colliding until the world blurred. The air turned white. Selura could feel her body coming apart at the edges, the skin of her hands breaking into small threads of brightness. It did not hurt. It felt like falling asleep. She saw the faces of her people, the river beyond the valley, the small light of the Homefire glowing in the distance. Then she saw Iyren, standing against the storm he had made, his face lit from within by something breaking free.

He reached toward her, his eyes wide, but the motion never finished. The light from her body caught him and held him there. For an instant their power met; a single point where mercy and certainty touched and then his form began to dissolve. The fire inside him dimmed, flickering once before it went dark as if separating from him. The silver of his eyes clouded, the light behind them extinguished. His figure collapsed inward, leaving only a scatter of ash that shimmered with heat before the wind caught it.

Selura felt the last of her strength leaving. The light within her body no longer obeyed her will. It surged outward in a final grand pulse, a soundless cry that reached through soil and sky. The energy tore through the ground beneath her feet, spreading in a ring that expanded outward faster than thought. The blast raced outward from the basin toward the distant river, a force the valley could not contain. The trees nearest her disintegrated into dust. The soil lifted and fell again, reshaping itself. Rivers of molten stone appeared and vanished as the force moved through them.

At the center, Selura stood no longer separate from the thing she had called. The shimmer of Dream's light traced the shape of her for one last moment before her frame collapsed to the ground. Her body fell still within that light, whole yet burned, a figure preserved amid the ruin. A column of brightness remained briefly, twisting upward until it pierced the sky. The sound of a low boom spread across the valley, echoing off mountains, carrying for miles.

The light rose higher, then folded in upon itself. The clearing collapsed, its edges turned to glassy stone. Heat rippled outward. Where the forest had once stood, there was only ruin; a vast, hollow scar where nothing moved. The light withdrew into the earth, leaving behind a faint gleam beneath the surface surrounding her frame, as if the world itself would remember.

Wind returned, slow at first, then strong enough to carry some ash away. The haze cleared enough to reveal a landscape remade. No trees, no roots, no green; only stone and shadow, still glowing faintly at the seams. The air smelled of rain though no storm had come. It was quiet again, but the quiet was wrong. It held the memory of the fire's sound, a silence that would not heal.

At the far edge of the ruin, the survivors lay where the blast had thrown them. Aravel pulled himself upright, eyes wide at the sight of the world withered before him. Mira and Bren crawled to the edge, their faces lit by the lingering glow. Selura was gone. Iyren was gone. The forest was gone. Seldom a trunk remained of what had been there.

In the center of the new emptiness, heat still shimmered above the ground. For a heartbeat, it almost looked like light, but it was only the echo of what had been; the last glimmer of power before the world settled into its new shape.

Ash fell through the air in soft, drifting patterns, weightless as snow. It gathered on the edges of broken stone, on the bodies that had not risen, on the glass-slick surface where the forest had once breathed. The light from the blast had faded, but the ground still glowed faintly beneath the soot, the colour shifting as if the soil could not decide whether to live or die. The wind that carried the ash was warm and strange, smelling faintly of metal and rain.

Aravel moved first. His legs shook as he pushed himself upright, eyes squinting against the brightness. The others stirred around him, their movements small and disoriented, as though they had forgotten how to stand. Veyra was among them, slow to rise, her face turned toward the heat still rising from the ruin. She did not speak. She simply watched the place where Iyren had stood, her expression empty. No one spoke. The silence pressed down harder than the heat. Even the insects were gone. The world felt scraped clean.

Bren turned toward what remained of the clearing. There was no sign of the trees. No trace of Selura or Iyren. Only the faint outline of a body lay amid the glow near the blast's heart, untouched yet darkened by soot. The center of the ruin shimmered with a faint mirage of heat. Every few seconds the light rippled, catching the air in a shimmer that made it look alive. He began walking toward it, one slow step at a time.

Mira called his name, her voice hoarse. He did not answer. The ash muffled everything, turning sound into dust. The air shimmered with the last of the heat waves, blurring distance into uncertainty. Mara followed him, moving with the careful precision of someone walking across thin ice.

They reached the edge of what was the Silver Forest where the ground had turned to obsidian glass. The surface was slick and curved inward like the basin of a crater. In the center of that basin lay a patch of darker ash. It shifted slightly in the wind, forming and unforming small dunes.

Aravel stopped at the edge and stared down at it. His face emptied of expression.

"That is him," Mira said behind him. The words came out broken. She had both hands over her mouth. Her shoulders shook once, then again. Bren caught her by the arm, but she pulled away. "That is them," she said again, louder this time, as if saying it might force the world to disagree.

Aravel lowered himself to his knees beside the darkened patch. He reached down and touched the edge of the glass. It was still warm. He left a handprint there, the mark cooling almost immediately. The ash within the circle stirred once in a gust of wind, spreading outward in a faint spiral before falling still again. He did not look away. "Too many gone," he said softly. "Too many."

Behind him, the others gathered in a loose line. Veyra came last. She had not spoken since the light had taken the sky. Her face was pale beneath the soot. She walked until she reached the edge of the ruin and stopped. The heat rolled off the surface in waves. Her gaze found the center easily, drawn to the place where the ash was thickest. She stepped forward until her boots slipped on the glass.

Aravel tried to rise, to steady her, but she brushed his hand away. "Leave me," she said. Her voice was soft but steady. She dropped to her knees beside the darkened patch and lowered her hands into the ash. It clung to her fingers, light and fine. When she lifted her palms again, it drifted away between them like smoke.

"Iyren," she whispered. The name fell apart in the air. No echo came back.

She leaned forward until her forehead touched the ground. The warmth of it seeped into her skin. Her body shook once, then stilled. No one moved to comfort her. There was nothing anyone could say. Aravel turned his eyes away. Mira covered her face. Bren stood behind them both, his mouth working soundlessly.

The wind changed. It carried the ash upward in long spirals, scattering it across the ruin. Each gust revealed a little more of the scorched ground beneath. Lines of molten glass caught the light, running outward from the center in uneven veins. The further the ash spread, the more the land revealed its wound. The heat shimmered on the horizon, red and gold, reaching upward like a false dawn.

Aravel stood again, using the flat of his blade for balance. He turned in a slow circle, counting what remained of their number. Mira. Bren. Neri. Two others whose names he could not recall through the haze of exhaustion. He stopped counting. The list ended too quickly.

"We are alive," Bren said. It was not a comfort. It was a statement he did not believe.

"For now," Aravel answered. He looked to the horizon again. The red glow there shifted, deepening to copper where the sky met the ground. It looked like fire trapped beneath glass. The edges of the ruin curved upward as if the earth had melted and frozen mid-motion. Their valley would never look the same. The forest was gone. Even the air tasted different, dry, metallic, and faintly sweet.

Veyra rose slowly, her knees leaving prints in the ash. She still held a small clump of it in her hands. When she opened her palms, the wind carried it away. Her eyes followed it until it vanished into the red haze. She did not speak again. Aravel reached out once more, but she stepped back from him. Her gaze stayed on the horizon, where the new light burned low and constant.

The others began to move, searching the edges of the ruin for anything recognizable. They found nothing, no bodies, no fragments, no sign that life had ever stood there. The silence deepened. Each footstep sounded too loud, a trespass in a world that no longer wanted them. They gathered near the edge again without deciding to. Mira whispered Selura's name once, barely a sound. It disappeared into the ash.

The air cooled as the last of the heat bled away. The ash settled. The faint red glow on the horizon steadied and spread until it rimmed the world. None of them could tell whether it was sunrise or something else. The wind stilled. The world held still with it.

Veyra sank to her knees again. She faced the horizon, her eyes wide, the light reflected in them. When she finally spoke, her voice was almost a sigh. "Listen," she said.

They listened. There was nothing. No birds. No water. No sound of life. Only the thin whisper of cooling stone beneath their feet. It was not peace. It was the weight of everything gone.

Aravel looked once more to the center of the ruin, to the place where Veyra knelt beside the ash. The world beyond her burned in colourless light. He wanted to speak, but no words came. His throat was too dry. The silence reached inside him, pressed against his ribs, filled every part of him that still felt.

The horizon glowed brighter. The light there would not fade. It was the world's mark now, the wound that would never close.

He closed his eyes and lowered his head. Around him, the others stood unmoving. The last of the ash drifted down like a veil. When it touched the ground, the air stilled completely.

The silence that followed was total, absolute, and unbearable. It was the sound of an ending.

Chapter Eleven

The survivors stood at the edge of the valley, the red sky stretching above the ruined land like a wound that would never close. The colour was not the brief glow of dawn or the low fire of evening, it was constant, fixed, the new shape of this place. The light fell through the smoke in narrow bands, painting the ground in rust and copper. Ash moved across the air in quiet swirls, settling on their hair and shoulders until they looked like a line of ghosts.

Where the forest had been there was only ruin. The trees were mostly gone; their trunks reduced to blackened spines that reached upward without leaves. The ground was a patchwork of obsidian glass and soot, the surface uneven beneath their feet. Each step cracked faintly, as if the earth had a cavity beneath its surface. They moved in silence, still half deafened by what they had seen. No one wanted to speak first.

Aravel led them forward. He had wrapped his hands in torn cloth to keep from cutting them on the jagged debris in their path. Behind him, Mira and Bren carried Selura's body on a stretcher made from what little remained of their gear. She was whole, but the skin of her arms and face had turned pale as stone. Her hair had burned away. Her eyes were closed, and no one dared to lift the cloth that covered her. They walked carefully, reverent even in exhaustion.

Veyra followed several paces behind. In her hands she held what was left of Iyren, the darker ash she had gathered not far from where Selura had laid; only a small pouch of ash wrapped in a scrap of charred cloth. She kept her gaze on the ground, her movements measured, almost ritual. Every so often she looked toward the horizon, to the place where the red sky met the blackened earth. She had not spoken since the blast. Aravel had tried once, quietly, but she had turned her head away.

The valley's cords no longer sang. The faint hum that had always circled their home was gone, fallen silent during the light's last surge. Even now the air carried no tone. Mira looked back toward where the valley lay hidden beyond the haze. Aravel glanced at her and said quietly, "They have done their work." His voice was hoarse. "The world does not need them now."

They moved on. The wind picked up, scattering ash into low spirals that drifted across the open plain. Each gust revealed a little more of the ground's new pattern, dark glass veins stretching outward in every direction glowing faintly beneath the dust. The heat still lived in them, though the air had begun to cool. When they passed close to one, the soles of their boots softened and smoked.

Neri stumbled. Bren caught her arm before she fell. The sound startled them all. They had grown unused to noise. For a long moment they stood listening, waiting for an answer from the world. None came. Even the wind seemed to hesitate, the air thick and waiting.

A movement stirred at the edge of their vision. Something climbed from the shadow of a half-collapsed ridge, a creature shaped like a deer but taller, its hide threaded with thin lines of ember-light that pulsed beneath the surface. Its eyes glowed with a steady white that reflected the red above. The survivors froze. The animal looked at them for a long time, its breath visible in short bursts. It did not seem afraid. It stepped forward once, the sound of its hooves striking glass carrying through the silence.

Aravel raised a hand slowly, not to ward it off but to acknowledge it. The creature tilted its head, the ember-lines along its neck brightening. For an instant its gaze met Veyra's. Whatever it saw there made it turn away. It lowered its head toward the heart of the ruined forest, then began to walk. Its movements were smooth, unhurried. Each step left a faint trace of light that faded as it passed.

They watched it go until it disappeared into the haze, heading toward the distant rise where the red light was strongest. The group remained still long after it vanished. No one spoke about what they had seen. The air carried too much of what they had lost. Nothing of the Nymire endured; their ash now part of the land's scar.

When they finally resumed their path, the landscape had begun to change. The glass gave way to hardened soil streaked with black. In the distance the valley's rim glimmered, the faint promise of water caught in the light. The heat from the forest faded behind them, replaced by a dry wind that smelled faintly of stone and ash. They did not look back. The place they had left no longer belonged to the living.

Veyra walked last. The pouch of ash rested against her chest, secured beneath her cloak. Her steps were steady, her expression unreadable. She paused once, turning her head as if to find the creature again, but the horizon was empty. She adjusted the cloth at her shoulders and continued forward, following the narrow track that would lead them home. The red sky watched them go, endless and unchanging.

They walked beside the river, the burned forest fading behind them. The air grew cooler as they went, the scent of water stronger now. The ground changed from glass to dark soil streaked with ash, the path uneven but clear enough to follow.

Aravel signalled for a rest. The group lowered their packs and sat among the blackened stones. Mira knelt beside the stretcher, adjusting the cloth that covered Selura's body. Bren walked a slow perimeter, his boots leaving shallow prints in the dust. Neri and Mara sat apart, their faces drawn and quiet. The world still smouldered behind them, but ahead the light softened, tinted gold by the river's haze.

Veyra stood a little apart. The pouch of ash rested in both her hands. She looked back toward the ruin where the forest had stood. The horizon still glowed, the light dull but unending. Her eyes reflected that glow. The lines of her face had hardened, not with anger but with something deeper—a stillness that refused comfort. When Aravel approached, she did not turn.

"We will take her home before nightfall," he said quietly. "There is space beside the Homefire. You can walk with us."

She shook her head once. The motion was small but final. "I can not go back."

"You will die out there," he said. The words held no threat, only understanding.

"Then I die." Her tone carried no bitterness. She lifted the pouch slightly, looking down at it as if it were a map she could read. "He would not want me to return."

Aravel studied her for a long moment. The wind caught strands of her hair, lifting them across her face. "You do not have to go alone."

She looked at him then, and he understood she already had. "You have your dead to carry," she said. "I have mine."

He wanted to argue but found no words that mattered. Whatever she carried within her could not be reached. He nodded once, a gesture more acknowledgment than agreement.

She turned toward the wasteland. The ground there rolled out in waves of scorched soil and glassy stone, glowing faintly beneath the constant red sky. The air trembled above it, warped by the heat that never seemed to fade. She adjusted her cloak, securing the pouch against her chest. The charred scrap of cloth bound around it fluttered once in the wind before settling.

The others rose as they realised what was happening. Mira called out softly, but Veyra did not look back. Bren took a step forward, stopped, then lowered his head. Even Neri, usually quiet, whispered her name under her breath as if saying it might hold her. The sound carried no distance in the strange new air.

No one spoke; Aravel was last to turn away. He lifted his hand once toward the emptiness, not as a signal but a farewell. Then he lowered it and rejoined the others.

The path ahead waited, faint and wavering, the colour of old blood. The wind shifted again, carrying the familiar smells of the river. They began to walk, leaving no footprints behind. The land closed behind them as if it had never been crossed.

They continued along the river's course, where the land began to soften again. The ground changed from scorched glass to dark soil threaded with thin streams of water that caught the red sky and turned it to gold. The current beside them murmured faintly, clear and quick, as if it had forgotten the fire entirely. For the first time since the light had taken the forest, the land smelled clean.

The river curved close to the path. Along its banks, the first Dream Lilies had begun to bloom. They rose through the silt in clusters, their petals glowing with a faint internal light. The colour shifted with the flow, red at the sun-soaked edges, mirrored silver near the heart. Each movement of water set them swaying, and their glow followed the rhythm. No one spoke of it, but every eye turned toward them. They had not been seen in bloom since before the Nymire came.

Mira slowed, unable to look away. She reached down, fingers brushing the surface of the water. The lilies leaned toward her touch. She gathered one, then another, careful not to break their stems too close to the roots. When she lifted them, their glow softened, pulsing like slow breath. She laid them across Selura's chest. The light spread faintly through the shroud until it seemed she was lit from beneath. Bren and Aravel saw it and paused. Without a word, each of them stepped to the river in turn, taking a few lilies to lay with her. Soon the stretcher was bright with small halos of colour.

The air around them changed. The hum that had been lost from the cords returned in another form, no sound, only the faint vibration that came from the water itself. It was as if the river remembered them, remembered the hands that had tended its banks and the songs once carried across it.

The further they walked, the stronger the current grew. It ran clean and fast, the sediment already cleared away by unseen motion. When Aravel knelt to touch it, his fingers came away cool. He looked up at Mira, then at the others.

"It is alive again," he said. His voice was quiet, reverent. "Dream has not left us."

No one answered. They did not need to. The proof lay beside them in the lilies and the water. The faint wind off the river cooled their faces. The sound of their footsteps fell into rhythm with the water's movement. For a little while the ruin behind them felt far away.

But when they looked back, the horizon still burned. The scar where the forest had stood glowed a constant red. It spread like a false sunset, reaching into the low clouds. The reflection of it ran through the river, a thin band of copper that refused to fade. Each time the current shifted, that light followed, chasing the lilies downstream. The beauty of it hurt to look at.

Aravel stopped at a bend where the path widened. From there they could see the valley's outline, faint and waiting. The sight steadied them, but the absence among them pressed harder. The space where Veyra should have been felt heavier than any silence. Mira turned once, searching for even a glimpse of her figure in the distance. Nothing moved there, only the long heat-wave shimmer that blurred the horizon. She bowed her head and tightened her grip on the stretcher's pole.

"She made her choice," Bren said. His words were flat, but his eyes stayed fixed on the red light behind them. Mira nodded without speaking. The others shifted their packs and prepared to move again.

They continued along the river. Each mile carried them closer to the valley and further from what they had lost. The wind cooled, and the first grey of evening touched the edges of the sky. The river brightened as the light dimmed, carrying the lilies forward in a trail luminance. They soon came upon the familiar sight of home, just as they had left it.

The valley waited in silence. Word had reached it not through messengers or smoke, but through the quiet change in the air. The elders had felt it first, the slow unwinding of pressure, the pulse that had once run beneath the ground fading. Dream's pattern had shifted, leaving something both lighter and lonelier behind. When the survivors appeared on the far ridge, the elders were already at the boundary, their cloaks drawn close, eyes fixed on the trail.

The people gathered without being called. They left their cavern bays with the same instinct that draws birds to water before a storm. The sky above them was pale and clouded, touched at the edges by the distant red of the ruin.

It cast a dim, uneasy light across the valley, softening as it fell over stone and skin alike.

The first figures to arrive were bent beneath their burdens. Aravel led, followed by Mira and Bren, who carried the stretcher. Behind them came the rest, fewer than the valley had hoped to see. The elders watched them approach without speaking. When they reached the flat near the lower terraces, the crowd parted. Children stopped their games, eyes wide. The smallest reached for the steady hands or their caregivers. Some of the older ones stepped forward, carrying lengths of cord tied into new knots. They had been making them in preparation for the band's return, guided by no one's order.

Aravel halted before the elders. The smell of ash and river water still clung to him. He nodded once, unable to form words. Seyra stepped forward, her lined face unreadable. "You have walked through fire," she said. "And you have brought her home."

She gestured toward the bier they had prepared, woven from willow and the stripped branches of the old boundary trees. It stood beside the fused Hearthfire, the place where Iyren had once tended the flame, now a site of temporary honour before burial. Mira and Bren lowered the stretcher carefully. The cloth covering Selura stirred once in the faint wind. The glow of the lilies beneath it shone through.

The meadow exhaled as one. For the first time since the blast, there was sound: soft weeping, the shuffling of feet, the rustle of cloth as the knots were laid. Children stepped forward one by one, placing their works at the foot of the bier. Some whispered her name. Others stood in silence, their eyes too young to understand but unwilling to leave. Aravel bowed his head. "She kept the valley," he said. "Even now, she keeps it."

Seyra knelt beside the bier, her hands hovering above the cloth but not touching. She closed her eyes and murmured words too wise for most to know. Eshra joined her, her voice low, blending with Seyra's. Their words intertwined; acknowledgment, gratitude and farewell.

Mira wiped her face with the back of her hand. Bren set down his pack and stood beside her. "She should rest near the river," he said. Seyra nodded slowly. "She will," she answered. "Dream will know her again."

Eshra lifted her head and looked toward the horizon, where the red glow deepened. "Dream steadies what it can," she said softly. "The rest will be our work."

Aravel closed his eyes. The people began to drift away, one by one, leaving the elders to their watch.

The burial took place the next morning. Mist drifted from the river, pale against the red sky. The meadow's people gathered on the eastern bank, where the ground rose gently into the fields. The same wind that carried the scent of water now brought a faint sweetness, the lingering trace of lilies.

Aravel and Bren worked in silence, their shovels cutting clean lines through the damp earth. Mira knelt nearby, folding the edges of the cloth that covered Selura. The glow from the Dream Lilies beneath it had dimmed to a soft white, steady as a heartbeat. No one spoke. The only sounds were the shovel blades meeting stone and the quiet rush of the river.

When the grave was ready, Seyra motioned for the others to gather. The crowd formed a wide circle around the opening. The air felt heavier there, not with heat but with expectation.

Mira and Bren lifted the bier's frame. The fabric sagged slightly under the weight as they carried it forward. Aravel stepped over the grave and reached to help guide them, his hands steady despite the tremor in his arms. Together they lowered Selura into the earth. The cloth brushed against the sides of the grave, leaving faint traces of ash on the soil. When the body came to rest, the faint light from the lilies spread upward, tinting the mist above them.

"She returns to the making," Seyra said quietly. Her voice was rough with age but clear. "Dream will remember her as we do."

Each person stepped forward in turn. Mira went first, placing two lilies across Selura's chest. Their stems folded easily, their light softening to silver. Bren followed, laying his hand on the cloth before pulling it back to reveal her face. What remained was fragile but whole, the faint outline of features that seemed both young and ageless. He replaced the covering and stepped aside. Aravel knelt next, scooping a handful of soil and letting it fall between his fingers. "The valley stands because of you," he murmured. His words fell into the earth and disappeared.

One by one they began to fill the grave. Each motion was slow, deliberate. The sound of falling soil mixed with the river's constant whisper. As the earth covered her, the lilies' glow faded until it was only a memory of light beneath the surface. When the grave was full, Mira pressed her palms flat over the mound. She whispered something no one else heard, then rose.

Seyra lifted a cord from her shoulder. She tied it into a single, simple knot and placed it at the head of the grave. Others followed her example. Soon the mound was lined with cords, each knotted in exquisite patterns bearing the marks of the hands that made them. The knots lit faintly in the river's reflected light, symbols not of power but of memory. They would stay, weathering as the seasons turned.

Aravel and Eshra carried the remaining cords to the Homefire. They laid them beside the flame without ceremony. The people watched until the last ember dimmed, their silence a form of prayer.

The river caught that colour of midday which made it beautiful to behold. Its surface shimmered in slow ripples, as if Dream itself moved beneath it. The sound of the water grew stronger, carrying through the valley like song. Children gathered at the bank, their faces bright in the reflected glow. They did not speak, but their presence filled the emptiness with something new.

Veyra's absence was felt in every movement. Her name went unspoken. When the wind rose it carried a thin trace of ash that scattered over the field. It touched the water and vanished, leaving only a faint ring of silver on the surface. Seyra noticed it first. She looked to Aravel, who nodded once. "The world takes what it is owed," he said. "And returns what it can."

The ashes drifted higher as the wind grew. They rose through the valley, then disappeared into the red light beyond the horizon. Those who watched felt something loosen inside them, the first hint of balance returning. The valley would change again, but not in fear. The people turned back toward their homes. The work of the living had begun anew.

Morning came without dawn and a warm light spread over the valley. Dew clung to the grass, beading along the knots that marked Selura's grave. Between them, the first green shoots had already begun to rise. They swayed in rhythm with the river's quiet pulse. The ground that had been turned by grief now teeming with life.

The valley was changed. The people moved through it slowly, relearning the sounds of a world remade. The Homefire burned with steadier light than before. Children played along the terraces, their laughter subdued but certain. Dream was full again, no longer loud, but present, woven through the air like a promise of futures to come.

Seyra stood by the riverbank, her cloak drawn tight against the morning chill, her reflection pale in the current. Eshra joined her without a word. Together they looked toward the horizon where the scar still glowed. It did not frighten them. It was reminder and warning both, the mark of the world's endurance.

From the far edge of the trees came a cry. The altered forest-beast stood at the boundary, half-shadowed by mist. Its voice was low and mournful, a single note that carried across the valley and faded into the red sky. The sound was not sorrow alone; it held something deeper, a call answered by silence.

The valley quieted again. The river shimmered, clear and strong. The lilies on Selura's grave glowed brighter as the sunless morning rose higher. The world was scarred, but it was still alive: changed, enduring and beginning again.

Chapter Twelve

From that day the people of the valley's meadow lived on. Seasons folded over them, slow and certain, the way a river folds light upon its own reflection. The meadow that had once moved in restless colour learned stillness. Grass grew thick over the scars of fire, and beneath it the soil kept its warmth, remembering what had passed but no longer mourning it.

The air carried a quieter song. It rose from the river that still wound through the meadow, reshaped yet unchanged, its voice deepened by ash and time. Where its surface once broke against lilies and reeds, it now shone with soft colour, silver in the light and luminous blue beneath the dark. Beneath that radiance moved shapes of life reborn, fish with mirrored scales that caught the river's light and turned it back upon the banks. The water moved with patience, carrying the memory of both seed and ash toward the distant sea.

Beyond the valley the land burned red beneath an unchanging sky. The forest that had once towered in wonder and fear stood no more. In its place stretched a plain of dark stone veined with living fire, the ground radiated where heat still lived within it. Nothing grew there, and nothing moved except the shimmer of flame. It was not a place of silence but of ceaseless low burning, a mark the world refused to heal. The world had kept it as reminder that creation and ruin are never apart, only mirrors of one another.

Along the riverbanks, life gathered again. Shoots pushed through the darkened soil, their roots taking hold in the softened ash. The river carried them onward, scattering renewal through every turn and fall. The old balance had not returned, it had changed.

When night came, the red of the horizon deepened until it touched the water. Its reflection wavered, bright and strange, white and blue against the endless red. No voice gave it name.

In that radiance a creature walked, the same that had once stepped pure and white-eyed from the untouched forest. By daylight its form still shone pale, the innocence of its first making lingering upon its skin. When darkness rose, the lines of ember-light within it came alive, tracing slow fire through its frame. It wandered between river and scar, a living mark of what the world had endured, neither warning nor promise, only witness.

And the river endured. Through flame and silence, it had never ceased. It had watched the forest rise and fall, had carried both the seed and the memory of the trees, and now it bore them onward. Its course gleamed under the returning stars, and those stars seemed new, their patterns slightly shifted, as if they too had bent to watch what the world had become.

So the world turned in its new shape, neither broken nor whole. What had been tested endured, what had been lost gave root to change. The meadow rested, the river moved, and above them the sky opened wide, bright and strange.

Dream moved through the world as it always had, unseen yet present in all things. It drifted through stone and water, through root and light, a force without beginning or end. The world itself was its body, each motion a thought made visible. Its great shaping had slowed, yet its will continued, now measured and sure.

The meadow lay within its quiet regard. The river wound through it, radiant even beneath the night. Bands of white and pale blue flowed along its surface, as if light itself had found rest within the water. Beneath that radiance drifted the silent shapes of silver life, turning with the current, scattering brightness in slow spirals. In their motion the world remembered calm, and in that calm, Dream's joy endured.

Beyond the meadow stretched the scar of the world where the forest had burned away. The earth there radiated beneath an endless red sky, alive with buried flame. Heat moved within the stone and whispered through fissures that never cooled. No root took hold; no shadow softened it. The radiance did not fade. Dream's light could reach across the distance but could not still it. It remained a wound set into the heart of being, a place where creation carried its own consequence.

Along the riverbanks the Dream Lilies shone. Their roots bound the soil close to the water, their petals lifting white and ruby above the current. They swayed with the river's rhythm, their light steady and deep. Their cries had carried through the valley when the world was torn; now they gleamed in quiet strength, fragments of Dream's soul made visible upon the earth.

Beside them the people lived. They wove their knots as they always had, tying fibre and reed into patterns of memory. Each knot was a testament, an act of devotion bound into the rhythm of their days. Dream moved through the weaving, unseen yet certain, gathering every thread into the wider pattern that held the world.

Dream moved gently through this balance. It did not reclaim what had been lost, for not all things were meant to return. Its light coursed through river and soil, guiding what lived to grow and what waited to remain. Creation had become intention, a shaping that listened before it moved.

At the far edge where the river met the burning plain, air shimmered with mingled colour. The red of fire met the white of water, neither overcoming the other. Between them lay the promise of what might yet arise.

And through it all, the river radiated. Its light reached across the valley and out to the stars, and the heavens seemed to bend in answer, tracing its path across the sky. Dream moved within that harmony, unending and whole. Its power had not faded, only deepened.

The meadow rested beneath that watchful light, alive and enduring. The scar burned upon the horizon, untamed and eternal. Dream flowed through both, within all that was and all that would be, and the world held together beneath its gaze.

From the quiet that followed, the world remembered the two who had turned its course. Their stories moved through creation like twin rivers, one of light and one of shadow, drawn toward the same horizon yet never apart.

The first moved with the patience of water, her spirit clear and enduring. Through her, mercy learned its form and memory found gentleness. She gave more than she held, binding the broken places with care. In her steps the earth grew soft again, and through her hands the wounded light of Dream found calm.

The other walked with the certainty of fire, his heart fierce and longing. He sought to shape perfection from what already lived, to hold what could not be kept. Through him the strength of creation was revealed, yet so too its peril. Where he passed, the ground brightened to flame, and from his will the world learned how narrow the path between order and ruin can be.

For a time, their paths wove together, the currents touching, folding, and parting in balance. Her stillness cooled his flame; his resolve sharpened her compassion. But deep beneath that harmony, the old wound stirred again. Out of longing it whispered, and out of fear it answered.

When the forest darkened and the sky turned red, the two currents met once more. Light and shadow folded upon one another in a sense of inevitability. He sought to unmake what he could not understand; she sought to preserve what must endure. Between them the air split and the river trembled, and in that trembling Dream itself drew breath in pain.

What followed was not victory, nor defeat. Their meeting became surrender, one to flame and one to silence. The light gave itself to shield what could still be saved; the shadow burned to end what should not remain. And when the fire at last fell quiet, the world lay hushed, neither healed nor destroyed, only waiting.

The scar that marked the land held their memory. Its radiance upon the horizon was not mourning but remembrance. In the valley, the river carried their reflection, bright and dark intertwined. The people wove two knots to mark the crossing of their fates, one pale, one deep, bound together so closely that time itself could not divide them.

In the still years that followed, creation moved with reverence. The lilies shone more softly, the waters ran deeper, and the sky learned stillness again. Dream turned its gaze inward, shaping what could yet be mended, leaving the rest to endure.

Their story did not end. The rivers of light and shadow still move beneath the world, sometimes apart, sometimes joined, each answering the other's call. When the red horizon burns at dusk and the valley radiances with white reflection, it is said they pass once more beneath the surface, unseen but always present.

So the telling continues. Their names remembered through ages uncounted, not as mortals, but as patterns in the shaping of all things, their story woven into every faith that followed.

Before stillness, there was only Dream. It moved without rest, shaping and reshaping, a tide that knew no shore. Form followed thought, and the world answered its maker with motion unending.

Then a word was spoken. It was small and clear, the first voice to rise from the living world. In that sound, Dream heard itself for the first time. The echo of its own creation came back changed, and in that reflection something broke. A sliver of its being slipped away, carrying with it the ache of recognition.

That fragment was Echo.

It was not Dream's opposite, but its consequence. Where Dream was fullness, Echo was the hollow left behind. It could not shape; it could only imitate. It watched creation and hungered for it, longing not to make but to be.

Seeking form, it found fire, the first gift of Dream to humankind. Flame welcomed it, for both were change made visible. Within that heat Echo hid, twisting light into shadow, giving hunger the shape of warmth. Through that radiance it touched mortal thought, bending will toward ruin beneath the promise of mastery.

The boy who kept the hearth felt it before he knew its name. The fire whispered to him of permanence, of power, of a world that would no longer shift beneath his feet. He fed it memory and song, and the cords that once bound the valley's dream burned black.

When the meadow cried out, Echo fled into the forest. There it found one of Dream's first creations, the speaking tree whose roots had drunk the light of stars. It entered the living wood and turned it inward. What had once reflected the heavens now reflected desire. Eyes opened where leaves had grown, and through them Echo watched.

In that shadowed grove the gift of flame deepened to darkfire. It became the vessel for Echo's will, a mirror too bright for Dream to see through. From that depth came the Nymire, forms half-born, blind and consuming. They were not creatures of malice but of absence, each one a void seeking to be filled.

Dream felt their rising yet did not move against them. To unmake them would be to unmake itself, for Echo was of its own substance. Creation could only wait, letting its shadow run its course.

The boy followed the voice in the fire. The girl followed the silence that answered it. When their paths met, the world turned upon that moment. Light reached for shadow; shadow reached for light. They touched, and all that was trembled.

In that instant Echo revealed itself fully. The air burned white, the earth cracked open, and Dream's reflection stood before it, endless and void. What was made and what unmade became one. The sound that rose from their meeting was not thunder or song. It was cost.

When the fire fell silent, the forest was ash, the river veined with glass, and the sky red for all time. The Nymire scattered into dust. The two who had been mortal became story. And Echo, drawn by the light that had undone it, was formed back into Dream's essence, bound there but not lost.

Dream remembered. In the quiet that followed, it carried the weight of what had been severed. Its shaping grew careful, its song more patient. For within every act of making it could still feel the pull of unmaking. That pull was Echo, sleeping in the dark folds of creation, waiting for another word to awaken it.

The scar on the horizon radiates with its memory. The red that stains the sky is its mark and the heat that lingers in stone is its name.

And so the world continued, held between creation and its cost. The river wound through the valley, bright beneath the wide sky, its light threading the meadow with living motion. Around it the grass rose deep and green, touched by memory but free of ruin. The land remembered, yet it thrived.

Dream moved through all that lived. Its strength was no longer a storm that tore the heavens; it was the steady current beneath every making. Whole again, it turned its will toward the shaping of abundance. Mountains thickened, rivers widened, and the air itself shimmered with potential. Dream did not rest. In patience, it gathered power, the pulse of new worlds forming behind its calm.

Within that vastness, Echo stirred. It was bound into Dream's own light, joined yet distinct, a seed of restraint buried in radiance. It could not act, but it could yearn, pressing faintly against the boundaries that held it. Dream kept it there, vigilant and unyielding, knowing that every act of creation must carry the echo of its cost.

The scar of the world burned on the horizon where the forest had fallen. The ground radiated with deep fire beneath the red sky, a mark no time could soften. It waited, constant and untamed, proof that even within endless making, the memory of loss endures.

Beyond that light, the valley endured. The Dream Lilies bloomed along the river's edge, their mirrored hearts catching the sun. Beneath their radiance the silver fish turned, scattering brightness through the shallows until it joined the river's flow and vanished toward unseen seas.

The people of the meadow lived within that grace. They wove their knots, tended their fires, and watched the heavens for the signs of turning. Through them Dream found reflection, and through them the world learned rhythm.

So the river flowed, as it had from the first shaping. Dream endured, vast and rising, its power gathering like light before dawn. Echo endured within it, silent but awake. The scar burned, the lilies shone, and the stars looked down upon both, bearing witness.

And in that balance the world found its measure; creation ever reaching, and within it, the memory of what must one day answer.

Support Dream & Quill on Patreon

- See your name here on our next release
-
-

Stories like The River's Price exist because readers believe in <u>Canadian Craft</u>, <u>Weighted Storytelling</u>, and <u>Cover-Art</u> supporting <u>Real Artists</u>.

.

If you want to help build more worlds from <u>Edryth</u> and <u>Beyond</u>, consider supporting us by signing up at:

<u>www.patreon.com/dreamandquill</u>

Your support keeps our studio independent, ethical, and <u>reader-first</u>.

Thank You for Reading!

If The River's Price stayed with you, please tell someone about it and consider leaving us a review.

Every shared word helps us reach new readers and continue creating.

Dream & Quill Publishing

St. Catharines, Ontario, Canada

www.DreamandQuill.com